SINGING

WITH **ALL**

MY **SKIN**

AND **BONE**

SINGING
WITH # ALL
MY # SKIN
AND # BONE

SUNNY
MORAINE

Undertow Publications
Pickering, ON Canada

undertowbooks@gmail.com
www.undertowbooks.com

TO ROB, ALWAYS

CONTENTS

IIIIIIIIIIIIIIIIII

SINGING

WITH ALL

MY SKIN

AND BONE

COME MY LOVE AND I'LL TELL YOU A TALE

||||||||||||||||||||||||||||||||||||||||||||||||||||||||||||||||||||||

TELL ME THE STORY ABOUT THE LIGHT AND HOW IT USED TO FALL through the rain in rainbows.

Tell me the story about those times when the rain would come and the world would turn sweet and green and thick with the smell of wet dirt and things gently rotting, when the birds would chuckle with pleasure to themselves at the thought of a wriggling feast fleeing the deeper floods.

Tell me that story, about how once we all had everything we wanted and never lost anything, about how once we slept and dreamed and sometimes we even slept without dreaming, total sleep that wrapped around our minds like a blanket and lulled and coaxed and woke just as softly, turning and sliding an arm around the waist of whoever happened to be beside you.

Tell me the story about lazy Sundays, about dinner at eight, about dressing like dolls and music that wound around us and kept out the world.

Tell me the story about how once there was cold, and snow, and all sound muffled and the world still, and a single one of those laughing birds sang tentative songs that suggested a long journey, a warmer climate, a finite amount of deprivation that only made the blooming of the world sweeter and more welcome.

Tell me about the times before the fires.

When you have told me that story, tell me the story about the time when we cared about false lives, little story lives within other stories, when we had time for such diversions, when we had the heart to care. Tell me about the shifting of flat light and faces and their trials and tribulations, how we suffered vicariously through them because their suffering made the beginnings of our own more bearable. Tell me about what it was like to grow up as an entire planet, to come to understand in our walled garden what everyone else already knew: that we were our own little diverting stories and that not all stories have happy endings. You and I both know they don't, but tell me about a time when we were still children, and ignorant, and we ran and played and didn't think about dying.

Sit down beside me in the dust and tell me stories of empire. Tell me stories of glory in war before the war came home. Tell me stories of wars in plays of light, rainbow light without the rain, and tell me all about how exciting it was and how we couldn't wait to see what happened next, all make-believe at being brave, until something else came along and stole our attention away. Tell me the story about how we really didn't think too much about it until those awkward family holidays, until looking without looking and then looking away, at scars and half a limb and perfect eyes that still stared and hated us for looking back. Tell me about how no one said anything. Tell me about that guilty silence, and about how we all felt like we were being jerked out of a dream and it was all our fault for having it in the first place.

Tell me stories about the first city falling, the running and the screams, blood-foam and trampling and how we watched it from so far away, so we still felt safe, mostly, but tell me then after that about how the helicopter hit the side of the building and bloomed fire, and then the tanks, and tell me about roadblocks and gunshots and how we didn't know what had been done so we didn't know how to keep it from happening to us.

On second thought, no, don't tell me. I don't like this story.

But I don't remember so I have to ask; won't you hold my hand and tell me about the highway and the curve of the mountain's back and the crystals of ice in the sky, a frozen rainbow like light that didn't fall but flew. Tell me about how our hands got so cold they were red and hurting, how we put them wet on each other's necks and screamed at the contrast.

Tell me about the times before all the houses washed away and you shot a man for a bottle of water, in the middle of a flood you did that, and I laughed because it was so funny how it made no sense but it made all the sense it needed to.

And then, once you've told me all of that, you can tell me about the hundreds of people on the roads, hundreds of thousands with bags and packs, with eyes like pits with little lanterns at their bottoms, and you can tell me about useless cell phones dropped and crunching underfoot like autumn leaves. You can tell me about when we had autumn leaves. You can tell me about fields of corn, green and gold, rough leaves that could scratch when they touched you in just the right way. Before all those fields were burning.

You can tell me stories about the dreams I used to have, sleeping curled against you in crude parodies of how we used to do, satire that never set anyone free but which still cut like knives. You can tell me about my dreams of wanting and comfort and plenty, of return, which you always said were pointless, when you told me to stop having them and I told you they were all I had, because then I felt like I didn't even have you anymore. You can tell me about the flat of your hand and my face and the moment when the two came together. You can tell me about the audacity of eyes devoid of the proper tears. You can tell me about the opening of a frozen space in time, a broken instant that marked the end of everything that came before and everything that came after. You can tell me stories about the real end of a real world.

But you can also tell me stories about everything before that spike of temporal ice. Please tell me stories about back when I had no idea what it looked like when a pregnant woman died. Tell me about when I didn't know what it looked like when a dog ate a child half-submerged in mud.

Tell me about the times before the camps, before the camps also burned, when we had beds, when we had sheets and their softness, and breezes that smelled like living and air. Tell me about the times before we got our food and our water from men and women in helmets, guns like pointing fingers and so angry, and at what? Can you tell me what they were so angry about? Tell me about when there was a time where no one told us what to do.

Tell me about the times before the stars were so bright.

Tell me about the times before the sun cracked and blackened skin, raised blisters and burst them. Tell me about a kind sun, a sun with which we could have love affairs. A sun we would travel thousands of miles to lie in, to stretch out in like cats, letting it touch every inch of us.

Tell me stories about blue.

Tell me stories about maps, about the discovery of terrain, about the luxury of taking our time. Tell me stories about adventures, about the joy of fine little shivers of imagined danger, about heights and sharp drop-offs that enticed us but which we never had to go near.

After that, tell me a story about the survival of how selfish we were. About how first it made us happy and then later it kept us alive.

But tell me about the first one.

Omit the latter, if you can.

Tell me the story about how that one time you said something funny, and it didn't matter what it was because it was funny, and I laughed, and you laughed, and no one cared that we were laughing and no one yelled to shut up or hit to make it so, and you put a hand on my belly and said soon, very soon now, and

I believed in *soon* as a concept. Tell me a story about when *soon* wasn't something to fear.

Tell me a story about when each second wasn't a needle's stab.

Tell me about when there were unbroken windows, about clear reflections, and faces you wanted to see, could admire, could improve. Tell me about polish and painted lips, and watching with half a smile, turning and moving for the sheer pleasure of seeing it so.

Lean against me and touch each of my fingers, one by one— the ones I have left, and the places where the lost ones aren't anymore—and tell me about before all the stealing, before the smashed storefronts, before we stopped standing in line for needless things.

Tell me a story about all the pretty lies.

Tell me a fairy story, a story with heroes. Tell me a story where virtue equals salvation. Tell me a story about a world where that matters. Tell me a story about being kind, not being weak and getting fucked over every time.

Tell me a story about a time that never happened, a thing we never did, like sharing what we had with the hungry-eyed people, the lantern-eyed people, looking at us like they'd kill us and take it all but then there was the gun so they never did. Tell me a story where we save people and they love us and we smile, yes, we did that and we were good. Tell me a story about how we might be good.

Tell me a story about back when we could be good. When we could pretend. Tell me a story about when *never* meant something more than *until*.

Tell me a story about when *meat* meant just *animals*.

Tell me a story about when you were whole.

Tell me a story about when there were still things I wouldn't do.

Please tell me a story about a time when this wasn't happening, when I wasn't crouching here by this fire and looking at you, touching all the places where you used to be, my belly empty and my head empty and all my memories running out of me like tears. Give them back to me, every one. I'm begging you, open your mouth and open your eyes and tell me about a time before the knife, before no choices, before being alone and starving and terrified and so numb that terror no longer matters, about no more lights but the stars, tell me about those pretty falling rainbows so I can look at them and not at you while I do what I have to do.

A story about the living taste of you, and about my mouth and your mouth and being consumed, and how greedy we were with each other. A taste that is not this taste and a greed that is not this awful, clawing thing twisting my gut into a devouring maw. An unkind thing. Less than you deserve and so much more than I do. Tell me about when I lived with you and not on you, not on your flesh and on your blood, and both so cold.

Tell me a story.

I need you to tell me a story so I can remember that this is not all there is, parting skin and no fat left and stringy muscle and thin blood, like water, in which I see no light at all. I need you to tell me a story so I don't die here, die and just keep moving anyway, slow and even all the way to the unhappy end.

I need you to tell me a story that isn't thicker blood in the dirt and loss that reaches into the heart and claws it out of your body. I need you to tell me a story about life and first breaths and cries that mean a future.

Tell me a story that isn't this story. I need you to tell it to me like stories still matter. Like they're more than whispers that die when the fire starts roaring.

I need you to tell me a story so I can put it in me and carry it with me, my own little lantern in the pit of myself, wavering and flickering but still lit, rainbows hiding inside it, on into the darkness without you. Tell me. Tell me all of it, to my teeth and tongue and throat.

Tell it to my belly, my heart. Tell me and I swear I'll believe you.

Oh my best beloved, tell me the story and I'll believe in the light again.

SINGING WITH ALL MY SKIN AND BONE

||||||||||||||||||||||||||||||||||||||||||||||||||||||||||||||||||||||||||||

I'M TELLING YOU THIS SO YOU KNOW: I DON'T REMEMBER WHEN I started eating myself.

You should remember something like that. It should be a moment, one of those that you carry around forever, a line that you cut across your life to mark *before,* when everything was one way, and *after,* when everything was different. I don't remember discovering it like a secret formula or an equation that explained the universe. I don't remember discovering it at all. I'm not sure it was discovery. I think maybe it was something that grew, that asserted itself, learning without meaning to learn, like walking or speech. You're made of things you can take to pieces, and those pieces can be eaten. The truth is that you're made of meat.

I do remember what I did with it. When I realized there was something to be done. I remember that very well. There's a world with someone in it, and a world without them. If it happens right in front of you, that's sort of hard to miss.

I carry these things around with me. I've been trying to say them for years, so if you don't mind.

There are all kinds of things you don't hear.

||||||||||||||||||||||||

What you need to understand is that this kind of magic persists because it works. It doesn't work in large ways, in obvious ways;

it's not showy and it's not out to impress anyone. This kind of magic is like a path through the night or tunnels beneath an occupied city, supply lines for resistance and the movement of agents. This kind of magic is the slender, fragile reclamation of power. When it's done right no one notices it's there. I've gotten very good at hiding it. But I was very clumsy, then, and even if it worked people saw too much of it, and that blunted its power.

It takes years of practice to know just how to destroy yourself. Just how much to pick away. Just how much to gnaw off. Just how much to cut.

What you need to understand is that I can't change anything. I couldn't protect myself then and I can't now. What you need to understand is that this has never been about anything but the sheer pleasure of survival.

⁙⁙⁙⁙⁙⁙⁙⁙⁙⁙⁙⁙⁙⁙⁙⁙⁙⁙

Here's what might have been the moment. It could have been any way, any time, somewhere between the number five and the number nine; it could have happened like this.

There's a healing scratch; the unevenness of it is pleasant, and the realization that fingernails slide so very neatly under its surface. It takes almost nothing to pull it away, and the blood wells up like liquid garnets, and it's so *pretty,* and there's something that washes over you then like slipping into a warm bath, and your breath comes easier, and you sag against everything.

And it comes to you that there's power in this, because just as you slip down, you slip *sideways,* and you see things you didn't see before. There are bones under the world, and now they're in front of you, and they rattle and dance. Grasses are deep jungles, streams are mighty rivers, here is the broken ground by a creek, and it's a massive gorge through which that river flows. Everything small is abruptly enormous and dramatic, and you can lose yourself in it. The sky flips sideways. Gods lurk in the branches and concrete and in all the machines, and polished stones whisper stories from when their melted hearts cooled, and they tell you everything they learned from their shaping rivers. You see everything that might be. You see the filthy, churning story factories. You see the eyes in the storm drains. Fuck your city-beneath-the-city bullshit, your vampire private detectives and your werewolves tending bar, because I've *seen* it.

You dig and dig, and suddenly there's a hole in you through which your spirit pours. You eat of your own flesh and drink of your own blood, and it's the deepest kind of communion.

And if they see you, they wait after school until you're ten minutes from home, and they pelt you with stones. What you've found can't protect you. But it seems like it just might be worth it.

⊦⊦⊦⊦⊦⊦⊦⊦⊦⊦⊦⊦⊦⊦⊦⊦⊦⊦⊦⊦⊦⊦⊦⊦

So there was that day when he followed me home from school, backed me into a corner of the afternoon, using his chest like a battering ram pulled back and ready to break through.

Put yourself here. See. It's amazing how everyone just disappears at moments like that. Crowded neighborhood full of kids headed toward home, but then the part of space you occupy is sealed off and it's just you and him, and you're bargaining, begging, dragging down the sleeves of your shirt, remembering that he came after you on the playground and feigned a kick to make you flinch, that he laughed and leered in your face, that you looked up at him and thought about the scabs on you like dinosaur scales. You thought about peeling it all away and revealing claws and pebbled lizard skin, and you thought about tearing his belly open with your toes and spilling his guts on the blacktop and screaming at the overcast sky while everyone else took their turn to run and the useless lunch monitors vomited against the wall of the gym.

Just a note: That was a spell that never worked. I did try. Don't think for a second that I didn't try. Even magic spun from torn flesh has its limits.

You make bargains in moments like that. I think we've all been there. For weeks, trying a variety of ways home, creeping along like a deer heading for water, ears and tail pricked. Never the same way two days in a row, but he found me, and I didn't understand exactly why it was so terrifying, being alone and small in that blocked-off space with him, but I offered him secrets.

Never mind what they were. Secrets are powerful. That's one thing I'm sure as hell not telling you.

He wasn't the only one, the first or the last, and when I talk about him I'm talking about them all, some of whom I remember and many of whom I've forgotten, but I've never forgotten what he said.

That's not enough.

Let's leave him for a moment. Let's take some inventory.

Match-heads work well. Just blow them out, press them against the inside of your arm—it's exquisite, though you don't get the satisfaction of feeding on the burns until after they've scabbed over. There's a pulse in the world, and you can watch it spread outward from those red, glowing spots, encasing you in a translucent shell. It never lasts, but it's better than nothing.

Unfolded paperclips work wonderfully, more slowly; the face of a wound parts like a smile and drools blood and clear plasma, and in that world that only you can see it steams like incense offered to a god. Gods respond to that kind of offering, and they gather silks and beautifully dyed wool around your heart. Clippers for nails, cuticles—these are delicate tools, a little too delicate and also a little too easy, because no magic ever comes without effort. They can make openings, beginnings, but then other things have to take over.

No needles or knives. They are too sharp, too clean. The best tools for this kind of work have edges that are ever-so-slightly blunted, that require commitment to use. Of course, fingernails are the best. They're always the best, ever-present and reliable, the claws I was born with even if they aren't the claws I wanted.

I'm telling you this so you know, but I'm not expecting you to be able to use this information. I can reach through this membrane and touch you, but I don't think you can really touch me. These are only scars to you, and all you ever saw was a strange little child who walked like a ghost through the world, looking for something without having the slightest idea what it was. More and less real both at once by virtue of spilled blood.

Ghosts don't bleed. I do.

<hr/>

They used to burn witches, didn't they?

<hr/>

There's something about skin, something supernatural. Not to say that it's magical or ghostly—though it is both of those things—or that it contains a power in and of itself, and that power magnifies when removed from a body—though it does. Skin is supernatural in that it *connects*, like a thin tendon, to everything part of but also *above* the natural. Skin is cells, hair, sweat, the potential of blood. Skin is sensation, an experience of what is. Skin is a lightning-spark network of a sensory organ, explicable and yet not at all.

Remove skin and see what's beneath. See how it all fits together. Understand the structure of something when that structure breaks down, and follow its slashing power lines to their source. I spun my first magic from the stuff of what I was, torn away because I could spare it. But I began because, like all of us, I had something I was trying to get away from.

Then I found other reasons.

<hr>

Let me tell you what I wish I could have said, when they saw the blood and the pits in my flesh and tried to get me to stop, because everyone knows little kids shouldn't do this shit to themselves. Let me tell you that when you discover a direct line into the fabric of the universe, it's very difficult to just leave that alone. Let me tell you what it's like to wear every mark like a secret ornament that only you find lovely, and to hate them at the same time because of what they'll mean to everyone else, so you hide them as best you can with long sleeves and shadows, but they always see in the end. Let me tell you what it's like to make blood magic, *real* magic, because packed under your fingernails the world loses its power to hurt you anymore. Let me tell you what it's like to run pain through a complex refinement process that makes it chocolate and warm sheets and dappled summer sunlight. Let me tell you what it's like to select your instruments of sorcery according to their sharpness and keen edges. Let me tell you what it's like to be a witch in junior high school. Let me tell you. Shut up and let me talk.

<hr>

I wish I could get this into words. None of them are coming out quite right. I want to tell you what it's like to have magic in your skin. Sit down beside me and let me illuminate all my scars, let me tell you all my many early names. No, they weren't bestowed like honorable titles, and they hurt worse than the actual wounds, but they dug into me just like everything else, and I have them still. Not all scars are the kinds you can see. Not all scars are beautiful. A changing body is a dangerous thing; a body that can be changed is more dangerous still. All these little bodies, all this potential, and imagine if they all found out how to take hold of it all at once. Every single beaten-down body, rising in angry flames.

God, we would have been terrifying. Can you imagine? Can you just imagine that? There's a reason why we send children off to war.

Here's one for the spell books: the potential of blood is sometimes more powerful than its presence. It's a fine line, drawn between intention and desire, but it's there if you know how to look. If you know how to walk along it, careful not to tip one way or the other. That moment before the capillaries rupture, before the pale flush of the fighter cells and the stacking of the platelets. Then there is a cycle of rebuilding, destruction, and rebuilding again.

Bodies are very persistent. They don't take no for an answer. If you can grab hold of that, it's like getting a tiger by the tail and teaching it to bring you the hearts of tender lambs.

That's not enough.

Okay, motherfucker, I'm enough. You know what? I'm enough. I'm the baddest bitch around, there's razorwire in my blood, I can clap my hands and summon an army of ravenous corpses from the cracks in the pavement, I can throw my tennis shoes over the telephone wires and turn them into a murder of hungry crows. I can spread my hands and break the world open, release one hundred thousand-eyed seraphs to see your soul to ruins.

I have a wolf's bite; I have a pack at my heels. My mothers were harpies and furies, my sisters were the Morrigan, my daughter will be fucking Kali. My grandmothers burned but saw me to birth in centuries of ash, and it doesn't matter that I always run away, and it doesn't matter that I'm trying to drive a devil's bargain with a grunting, sweating fifth grader, and it doesn't matter that you made me cry all those times before, because you think I'm not enough? You piece of shit? I can roll up my sleeves and tear off my skin and make you fucking *cease to exist.*

That could have happened. It could have.

I'm telling you this so you know.

<hr />

What I won't tell you is whether or not they ever found him. I won't tell you if it happened all at once or little by little, slowly enough for him to scream as he lost his limbs, his heart, his tongue. I won't tell you whether I cried at what was happening or just watched, impassive, or whether I laughed and clapped my hands. I certainly won't tell you whether or not I ran away. I certainly won't tell you if I bargained in the end. I won't tell you if it all failed, if I can only look back and rage, if I'm just lying to myself even now and all I have left is stories and those lies and where my feet could take me.

We're always making bargains, is the thing. We forget them, but they happen. Secrets for life. Flesh for power. Blood for knowing. No one had to teach me these things. I learned them from being in the world. But even if you don't ask for something like that, it has a price.

<hr />

I don't curse crops. I don't cause children to be born sickly or deformed. I don't bring plagues of rats. I've never stolen the breath of a baby while it slept. I can't travel in chill night winds. I can't give you a potion to catch the heart of your true love. I can't read the stars, and I have no idea what's going to happen next. There are all kinds of things I can't do. I count my marks and take stock of my little magic, my flesh-and-blood magic, and I think I only have so much of both to give.

And I've given a lot to get this far. But I'm still here.

And I'm telling you this so you know.

A PERDITION OF SALT

IIIIIIIIIIIIIIIIIIIIIIIIIIIIIIIIIIIIIIIIIIII

I LIVE IN WET. I FALL ON YOU.

Consent doesn't enter into this. I come whether you want me to or not, because I obey the impetus of gravity and I am constrained by the basic chemistry of hydrogen and oxygen. I fall and I can't help the falling, though I never scream. You, always believing you could somehow dart between the drops, laughing and running for the shelter of awnings, doorways, bus stops, et-cetera. You never carried an umbrella. You said they were cumbersome. I laughed at you. I followed your lead. We got soaked together.

So in a way this is perfect when you think about it.

IIIIIIIIIIIIIIIIIIIIIIIII

There is no waking up. That's the thing they don't tell you, not that they ever really tell you, or at least they don't tell you that it'll be like this. Not non-existence. But you always expect an existence that feels familiar, that you can make sense of. There is no making sense of a sentient liquid state. It's like something you'd find in another world, a being so impossibly strange that you would simply regard each other in incomprehension, and then maybe the liquid being would flow over you and dissolve you for nutrients.

I think about dissolving you, floating in my clouds, floating as my vapor. I think about turning you into something like me, incorporating your molecules into mine. We used to connect on that level, I thought. I used to plunge into you over and over, I used to lose myself inside you. It was stupid and romantic and I never trusted romance at all, but I swear to God, I swear, I could reach into you and close my hands around your heart.

There are rules. I can only ever touch your skin, your hair. When I'm lucky I can flow into your eyes until you rub me away. I can be inhaled by accident and make you sneeze—it's gross but it's worth it. I can touch your tongue, the backs of your teeth— how do I taste? It must depend; my exact composition varies. I can extend myself into your throat, I can feel your heat and your wet and I can be part of that. For such a short time, I can be inside you again.

Three days of rain. An unusually wet spring. Left on a lazy weekend with nothing much to do, you stay inside and plumb the depths of the horror section on Netflix. We worked through the best ones together and at the end all we had were the dregs, the absolute worst of the worst, but we watched them anyway because I wanted to, because even the awful stories were a distraction and everything else just seemed so weirdly maudlin.

You watch them now and you begin in the pajamas I gave you last Christmas (warm and fuzzy, the kind of pink that stabs you right in the eyes) with a bowl of popcorn but you end in tears, watching the last of the sorority girls on an ill-advised spring break road trip getting slaughtered by the man gone mad in the remote cabin. She dies with an ax to the forehead in a state of utter surprise. She thought she was free and clear. I think I used to love these movies because I could actually grasp how everyone felt. The killers. The dying. The dead.

You watch her die and you weep in your fuzzy pink pajamas.

You're not even looking at the screen anymore. You look at the window, the one I'm beating myself against in a hard, gusty wind, wanting to penetrate the glass and get at you. I look at the tears on your face with open jealousy. Salt, distant sister to the sea; I know her, I've spent time in her, I've left her again. Now I envy her but there's nothing I can do. No one else should know the exact circumference of your eyeball the way I do. No one else should get to kiss the corners of your eyes.

Later I watch you in bed with both hands working between your thighs, I see the gleam of wet slick on your fingers and I fucking hate it. I'd kill it if I could. That should be me. Every drop of it should be me.

⁘⁘⁘⁘⁘⁘⁘⁘⁘⁘⁘

I never get to be your shower. I don't know why. There are certain places that are closed to me. I can be the droplets of condensation on the mirror, on the tile, I can see your foggy outline through the frosted glass, I can see you when you step out, the sheen on your skin. But I can never be that water, flowing over you. I can't even be the steam that's closest to you, rising off you like an aura. I can be the rain, I said that, but that isn't the same. I can be inside you for that briefest of times, but that's not the whole of what I want. We used to stay in there until the hot water was long gone, and it wasn't even about sex; it was just being together, the sensation of skin on skin. It was fascinating, and now it's lost to me.

I learned, in those final days, that we never really touch. That it never happens. That we feel it, but the truth is that our atoms repel each other and the nuclei never come into contact at all. The stuff that we are never meets. We come so close, but always physics stops us.

I look back on that and on everything that's denied me and I think I'm in a kind of hell. Endless falling and rising and falling again, teasing fragments of the utter unity I dreamed might be ours eventually. I never believed in any kind of afterlife, I used to find the idea of nonexistence weirdly comforting, but fading out on that hospital bed, I was weak, and I wanted so much to believe.

And I was right.

And it fucking sucks.

I don't dream, but I *think*. I'm a thing of memory. I exist in the now, but I can't even begin to imagine an actual future of this, so when I time-travel—figurative, of course, always—it's backward.

If I could have been this, then. If I could have gotten free, even for a little. If I could have looked away, stopped watching you watch me, stopped feeling your hand on my chest, rising and falling a little lower every time. I wanted to wipe your tears away but by then there was so much morphine that I couldn't lift my hand. *Pain management*, God, they weren't managing anything; it's a slow death to make the big one more bearable. For whom? Whose pain was being managed? It felt like betrayal. I didn't want you there. For all those surgeries, all that blood getting sucked away, all that blood that had turned against me, for the nights in and out of the bathroom, the stink of the vomit that we both stopped smelling after a while. Tubes and bags full of poison the color of piss. Actual piss. All those fluids that run through a body. All that wetness, because bodies are mostly wetness; we die soaked in ourselves. We die that way and then little by little we dissolve unless we burn and hiss and pop into vapor. And before then they pull out that wet, drain and tidy up, and put in their own.

I was invaded, over and over again. I was torn open, riddled full of holes; I was a sagging bag of nothing by the end. And you fucking *watched*, you bitch, I *told* you to stop and you just wouldn't even do that much for me.

I loved you so much and you wouldn't leave me alone.

⦅⦅⦅⦅⦅⦅⦅⦅⦅⦅⦅⦅⦅⦅⦅⦅⦅⦅⦅⦅⦅⦅⦅⦅⦅

Maybe it's you. I think about that after a while. I settle in the folds of your hair, I nestle into your scalp—close to but never actually part of the minute beads of your sweat—and I think about what might be keeping me here. And yeah, it could be me, because I was always the kind of person who hung onto things, who could never throw away letters or postcards or emails, who held onto books long after all chance of rereading them was gone, and you always used to complain about our full DVR. I don't let go. It could be me. It could be the final logical extension of a lifetime of an iffy habit.

But it could also be you.

I watch you for any sign that you miss me. If you linger over Facebook statuses. If you ever go back and look at stuff on my Instagram from weeks before we got the diagnosis, before we got hit by that first merciless wave. You got rid of all my clothes, and I tried not to be hurt by that, but you do go back to those little incorporeal digital artifacts of me. When we die the parts of us that exist in those spaces are abandoned, and we know they're abandoned by the fact that they remain unchanged. People left messages on my wall, but there's nothing new there of me anymore. That side of me is a series of mausoleums. You wander through binary tombs.

I see you holding on in your way. How hard? I would trickle through your fingers if you actually tried to grasp me, but there's more than one way to do that. There were those times in the shower. There were the messages I left on the mirror in steam. We met on the beach; I had beads in my hair. For our honeymoon we went to the coast and soaked ourselves in an ocean without a memory.

This has defined us. I am what we always were.

There are stories about people who make it out of hell. There are stories about people who go into it voluntarily. For some reason there are a number of stories about people who take day trips there. There are stories about people who are purified, who are cleansed, and who, having performed various tasks congruent with processes of redemption, are finally allowed to ascend.

I already know that can't happen to me. I already ascend. Over and over, I rise and fall. There's nowhere to return from. There's nowhere to go to.

But I'm trying. I am.

So I know the moment I feel peace, peace which is a kind of aggrieved resignation, but then something else happens. I know the moment when I let go of not letting go. I know the moment when I run through my own fingers.

We met on the beach. I follow you there in the rain, its return, kissing every inch of you, trickling under your clothes. I taste the salt of you, and again I make you and me and the sea a circle of sisters, three graces dancing under a gray sky.

Your feet hit the sand, the gulls scream, and you pull off your shoes. It's not gentle vacation sand; there are rocks, there are pebbles, but you run forward on bare feet, and as I cling to you and the flat slate of the water spreads out in front of us, crashing foam, I remember what you did with me, I remember that you threw me into this, when I was dry, when the fire had sucked everything out of me. I forgot it, it was the antithesis of what this life after life has become, but I touch it and you again, and the combination brings it all back. It was raining that day, too. It was raining and you were alone and crying and everything was so *wet*. Showers of dry white ash on the waves. On your hands. The wind turned and fragments of me scattered across your face, your hair.

You put me here.

You run and I hold on, which is what I've been doing, which is a promise, which is what death is, and when you plunge into the waves I come with you. You're on your hands and knees and you paddle and crawl into the deeper water, your white summer dress heavy and lank and then swirling around your legs, making a mermaid's tail. It's cold but every part of you is burning the water to steam. Or it would be. It would be if the world were fair. You'd be sending me back to the sky.

You throw your head back and laugh, and just as you do that the water rushes into your mouth, and for a few seconds I'm outside of you and inside of you and in your throat and belly and eyes and hair and nose, your ears, I could whisper and scream even if you forgot how to hear me. It's perfect and I don't want it to stop because it's what I needed, what I was waiting for.

But then I touch the soft damp folds of your lungs and I know I can't.

You're fighting me. But I link hands with my sister the sea and I *shove* at you. You go flailing, and you're hurled at the shoreline in a burst of salty foam, prone and scrambling, my own Venus emerging from the waves. My own new life testing limbs, dragging in that first fatal breath of air.

Stay.

I don't wait to see you pushing yourself up. I don't need to see that. There are some things I shouldn't see, and we can still make these choices, though I'll never know if they're the right ones. Now I let the tide carry me out. I let myself float, buoyed upward. We had a spring of rain and now the summer heat is coming.

COLD AS THE MOON

||||||||||||||||||||||||||||||||||

BEFORE THE SUN WENT DOWN DADDY BECAME A BEAR AND RAN AWAY over the ice floes.

I didn't see him go. I stood in the doorway and I looked out at the sun hovering close to the horizon, the sky like a huge milky half-closed eye. I pulled the blanket closer around my shoulders and I tried to will myself to cry but nothing came. It seemed like something I should do, cry for a daddy who's gone and who left us without saying any kind of goodbye, but instead I took a breath of air so cold it ached in my lungs, turned around and went back into the house, closed the door behind me and went to the kitchen and stared at the last of our powdered eggs.

In the next room, Carol stared crying. It was a weak little sound. It made me think of the wind trying to get in through the old weather stripping on the windows. I sat down at our tiny table and I looked down at my hands like they might make more sense than the eggs, the cracks in my knuckles, the backs all raw and red.

I have no hair on my hands. Never have. Isn't that something?

||||||||||||||||||||||||||

You think you might be able to see signs that your daddy is becoming a bear. You live with him through a winter of night and a summer of day and another, and you think you know him, but you don't know that he'll be a bear one day and run away from you, big paws padding over the ice and snow. You watch him dine on seal meat, and maybe he likes it very, very rare, rare enough to be bleeding, but for some reason you don't think there's anything abnormal about that. You hold Carol on your knee and feed her hydrated dehydrated mashed potatoes and you tell her stories about Mama and her face and hair and eyes and the way she'd laugh until Daddy slams his fist against the table and tells you to stop.

You used to think about walking away, about running but you stayed, because someone had to, because someone had to be human, because you thought there might still be some love buried deep down with the rot, and finally because you hated, because hate binds tight and cold as chains.

I say you'd do these things because I did and I swear you would too. In my place. In my place you might do all sorts of things you'd never believe you were capable of. Never is not a real thing. You would. I'm telling you, you would.

||||||||||||||||||||||||

Carol lies on her back and waves her fists, but she looks like she's struggling against something instead of fighting it. Like she's losing. The light comes in so thin, the way it will be for the next four months when it's here at all. I look down at Carol in her tiny crib, and I think about what things were like before Daddy was a bear and Mama was still breathing and walking around. Carol used to be a fighter. She fought her way out of Mama's belly is what Daddy always said. She was like a boxer from the moment she was born, her fists up, shielding her head. Little Carol came out swinging.

Little Carol is down for the count.

I lift her in my arms and she feels so light. I hold her against my shoulder and I carry her back to the kitchen. I lay her down on the table and I go to the hotplate with my powdered eggs, and I get some water and I stay here and I do what I have to do.

⁙⁙⁙⁙⁙⁙⁙⁙⁙⁙⁙⁙⁙⁙⁙⁙⁙

Daddy never claimed we could live on canned food and dry everything but I think he really did sort of believe it when he dragged us up here. Daddy never explained his logic, maybe because he thought it was self-evident. And it was, I guess. I mean, I could understand it, with my gut even if I couldn't get it with my head.

I found Mama, her face all blue inside the plastic. There was vomit crusted on her lips. She pissed the bed. Death is so fucking ugly, I said later to no one in particular. I never really thought it could be so ugly. Something that ugly spreads like cancer, like the cancer that was eating her from the inside out. The ugly death that got her was already inside, her, or at least I think that's how she felt, and all that happened was she picked the time and the way it showed up. But once it wasn't inside her anymore, it spread out and infected the rest of the world. Mama gave the whole damn world a cancer.

Mama had her cancer when Carol was born but Carol came out the most beautiful thing I had ever seen. Carol came out clean.

⁙⁙⁙⁙⁙⁙⁙⁙⁙⁙⁙⁙⁙⁙⁙⁙⁙

After, Daddy said he was tired of all the damn heat. Said he wanted a change.

Everything anyone does has a logic to it. That's something I know. So I don't ask why. It's a pointless question. *When* and *how* are much better. Mama answered those. Daddy became a bear and he answered them too. I haven't decided how I'm going to deal with them on my own.

Carol doesn't eat the eggs. She cries, spits them up when I try to push them into her mouth with the spoon. A week ago we ran out of formula. A week and a half ago the gas in the snowmobile was gone. I don't even know how—it was just gone. If there's a logic to that I haven't found it yet, but Daddy always said that sometimes shit just happens.

Daddy didn't say it about the formula or the snowmobile, but I could tell he was thinking it. Daddy, Daddy, just tell me we're going to be all right.

Daddy says I won't lie to you, Susan.

Fuck you, Daddy. Just fuck you. Daddy, we can't all be bears, can we?

I can't do it anymore, said the note Mama left. That was all. She didn't say what she couldn't do. She didn't say why she couldn't do it. That was her logic, her reason. She did what she did because for her there weren't any options left.

She left. She busted loose the chains, the cage, got free. I wanted to envy her, later. I didn't know how. I still don't.

The sun goes behind the horizon again and Carol is whimpering now, and I like that she's quieter and I feel guilty for liking it because I know it's because she doesn't have the energy for those normal, full-voice cries. I put her in the basket Mama wove for her, sitting in the sun room all those spring afternoons, and I look at her and the painting on the wall that I did for eighth grade art class. I won an award. It's ugly, too. Mama liked it and since she did what she did I've stayed up nights wondering why.

It's a landscape. It's wide and open and the sun is shining, and there are rolling hills and wide fields below the hills and a little bunch of trees on the right. The perspective is fucked up, but not as bad as you might think an eighth grader would do. The grass and the trees are green and cheerful. The clouds are done pretty well—I was always most proud of the clouds. I hung it up here in the little closet that passes for our living room because it was something that was a window to what we had before all the ice and the months of night. I always got the sense that it bothered Daddy but he was nice enough to not tell me to take it down.

But it's ugly. It's ugly because it's impossible so it's a kind of taunt. I can't go there. I don't think that place ever really existed.

I reach down and I lay a hand on Carol's chest, feel it rise and fall. Feel the flutter of her heart, like the rapid-fire of a scared little hamster. I don't take my eyes off the painting, and in the shadow thrown by the trees I'm suddenly sure I can see a bear crouched, looking out at me with black holes for eyes.

⫸⫸⫸⫸⫸⫸⫸⫸⫸⫸⫸⫸⫸⫸⫸

I could tell Mama didn't want Carol. She never said it, but I could tell that she wasn't happy along with her surprise. She spent weeks making that basket, but to me it felt like she was arguing with something. Like she was making it to prove a point. She would sit in the sunroom and Daddy would sit in the den and they wouldn't talk to each other.

Not talking to someone like that isn't just not doing something. It's *doing* the not-doing. There's just as much behind it as there would be if they were screaming in each other's faces. I didn't get that while it was happening, but before Daddy became a bear that's what we were doing to each other a lot of the time.

Daddy, maybe if you had just talked to her.

Daddy, I really tried to not resent you. But now you're a fucking bear. How exactly am I supposed to feel about everything?

I could sing to Carol. I pull her into my lap and I do, soft and gentle, like I remember Mama doing for me. Thing is, I remember Daddy doing it too. They both sang, and sometimes it was a duet, and before I could even talk I remember it was so beautiful that I cried. A baby, crying not because she's hungry or tired or because she's shat herself but because something hurts in her heart.

We shouldn't be able to feel those things before we have the words for them.

Hush little baby, I sing. Daddy's here, Mama's here, Mama's not dead and Daddy's not a bear. The sun will come up and the ice will melt and we'll have flowers again. And food. We'll have so much food, you'll eat until you're sick and you'll eat some more.

Carol shivers against me and closes her eyes. Her thumb finds its way between her lips.

Lies are the only things in the world that aren't ugly.

You have to be strong, is what Daddy said after the funeral. He sat me down on the porch and he looked very serious, but all I could think was that I hadn't seen him cry, and I didn't believe anything he said at the funeral about love or losing it, and now I couldn't escape the feeling that he was saying these things because they made sense to say but not because he really felt them.

I'm counting on you, Susan.

In the house, in the front room behind the screen door, Carol started crying. Daddy looked up and then I did see the tears in his eyes, and they weren't fake, and I felt sorry. Just for a moment Daddy looked sadder than I had ever seen him. More than sad;

Daddy looked *lost*, lost and like something was chasing him. Something with fur and claws and teeth.

She's gone, Daddy whispered. Oh, God, she's really gone, isn't she? How does that even happen?

I said, Don't you know? And as soon as I said it, I knew it was just about the least useful thing I could have said. But it was too late, and for a moment Daddy was twice as big in his black funeral suit, and fuzzy at the edges, like for a fraction of a fraction of a second he wasn't quite real.

I got up and went in to Carol. Someone was counting on me. Maybe it was Daddy and maybe it wasn't.

I don't think Daddy is counting on me anymore.

I was so happy about Carol. I always wanted a sister. I was going to do sister things with her, and I was going to have someone to tell my secrets to. I was going to have an ally, someone to watch my back. I was going to watch hers. Her little fingers and toes and brown fuzz-hair and her red, scrunched-up face were so completely perfect.

I was the only one who was happy about Carol. It didn't really bother me, not then. As long as someone was.

So Carol dies.

So that happens.

I think about Daddy as a bear. I think about him loping across the snow, across the moonlit ice. In my mind, Daddy isn't a polar bear—which would make a lot of sense up here—but a grizzly, huge and shaggy and brown. Daddy has long, lethal claws that can scrape pits in the ice. Daddy can rear up on his hind legs and blot out the sky. Daddy has teeth and with them he gnaws at the world.

Daddy never sleeps.

I think about Daddy's fur, how it might be soft, the only part of him that is anymore. I think about curling my hands into it, gripping big, thick tufts, climbing up onto his massive shoulders and letting him carry me into the dark. Just me, all alone. I think about Daddy roaring at the moon, everything that he came up here to freeze into silence bursting at last out of his hot, stinking throat.

How do I know Daddy is a bear? How do you know anything? I look back on everything that's happened up until now and really it's the only thing that makes sense.

|||||||||||||||||||||||||||||||

Carol's little body is getting cold. I hold it to my chest and I rock her gently, humming a song that I know I'm fucking up because I barely remember it anymore. Songs are for my dreams; music gives Daddy a headache. Or it did. Since we got here, no music at all, except low under my breath with Carol close to me, singing it in her little ear on just a whisper.

Carol is so small; somehow she feels smaller than when she was born. The thing that ate Mama followed us here and ate her too. Carol's death is just as ugly in its way, but here in the dimness with her head on my arm, she looks like she's sleeping. A little. I've heard people say that about dead people but it's never true, is it? A dead person is just a thing. You can tell just by looking.

I can't think of Carol as a thing. I just can't do that.

I can't do it anymore.

I get up. I'm still wearing my parka—it's got to be less than forty degrees in here by now. I pull up my hood with one hand, fumble for my gloves with Carol still held tight in my other arm. Somehow I get them on without laying her down, and I find a blanket to wrap her up in, keep her for a little while from the cold. I think, there are some things that are just completely pointless and you do them anyway. It's not even a matter of habit. It's a matter of doing the things you did when you were sure you were alive.

So I walk outside and the moon is rising. I'm walking away but I'm still not leaving. In my arms, Carol is a little bundle of carved ice. I sing to her and the wind, soft and mournful, sings back.

So at least someone is sorry.

ııııııııııııııııııııııı

Daddy, you were always a bear. You were always furry and wild and you never liked walls, so of course when you put us inside walls so close together you couldn't stay inside yourself anymore, you burst out, you had to run. I don't even really blame you for it. You're just what you are, Daddy, and so is everyone. But I am what I am, and I don't have your fur. You never gave that to me, and you sure as hell didn't give it to Carol, who's stiffer and stiffer in my arms as I walk, up to my knees in snow.

Daddy, I have a knife on my belt. I think about cutting your throat with it, skinning you to make a blanket that I can wrap around Carol and me. All stinking with blood and the sweat of a bear. All stinking with being kept inside a tight bear skin for way too long.

Daddy, before they took Mama away on the gurney I swear I saw claw marks under the scarf around her neck.

ııııııııııııııııııııııı

I stop when the moon is high. The wind is picking up now, not just those little whispers and sighs but a full-on scream, like Carol used to do when she was so hungry and no one was picking her up, like I used to do with my face pressed into my pillow, screaming until my face ached with it. Right now I'm quiet, and I let all that noise settle between my ears, and for some reason it actually calms everything down. Ahead of me there's a little rise but there aren't any trees that I can see, the wind kicking the loose snow up into a mist, giving the moon a halo with the faintest kind of rainbow shimmer.

Top of the world, Mama. I thought that over and over on the drive up here, running on a loop through my brain like a song. Top of the world to you, Mama, you pile of charcoal and ashes. Top of the world to you, Carol, you stiff little ice cube. I'd hold up your fist and declare you a winner anyway, except I have a feeling that your arm would snap off in my hand. Top of the fucking world to you, Daddy, you bear. You coward and you bear.

You just couldn't keep it in, could you? You just couldn't stay in your cage.

<hr>

Seated in the snow, I watch Daddy come over the ice floes.

He pads along on all fours like he weighs nothing. Even far away I see his fur ripple as he moves, its gloss in the moonlight, the snow on the wind making him look like the idea of a bear rather than the real thing. Daddy comes back, and I hope for some kind of apology, holding my dead sister in my arms, but I don't really expect to get one, because when have bears ever apologized for anything?

Bears are bears. And I'm me. And Mama and Carol are still dead, and it's just us now, according to this big hard logic that carves lines through the world and divides you up like a fifth grader dissecting a frog. Cuts you up and catalogs.

Daddy ran out of options and then he ran away.

But now he comes back.

I stand just before he reaches me. His eyes are pits in his head and he snorts, shakes his muzzle, lets out a growl that sounds a lot more like a groan. Like he's in pain. I stand and I stare back at him, and I hold Carol out to him like a present. Take her, you bastard, I say. Take her like you never could, not you or Mama. Take her and let this be over.

He snuffles at her. Curls back his lips. Moving so carefully, teeth shining yellow, he closes his jaws around her tiny body, tips his head back, swallows her without chewing. Swallows her whole, undamaged. Gentle. I watch this happen and at last I feel like I can cry, like it's my choice.

But I still choose not to. I could have walked away. I choose not to do that, either. I've been making that choice, over and over. It's become my logic. Maybe I never could have chosen anything else.

Daddy shakes himself again and looks at me. His eyes should shine like his teeth, but they don't. When Daddy wore his human skin, his eyes shone, because it was all the bear packed into him and looking out of the world. But now the bear is all there is. There's nothing to shine. He's all stretched out, inflated, empty inside like a balloon.

Daddy rears up onto his hind legs. I raise my head, but I don't turn. I don't run. Whatever else happened or didn't happened, no one ever hurt me with hands, and I don't think anyone will hurt me with claws now. Daddy, I know why you came up here, but why did you bring us? You got rid of Carol in the end. Did that feel good? Are you relieved? What were your plans for me?

Did you have any?

I still think maybe I could have left. Instead I'm here. Just you and me, finally a chance for some quality time. It's become a matter of some kind of principle because that's literally the only thing I've got left.

Except you.

Daddy sways, growls again, and drops back to his forepaws

with a hard *whuff.* He noses at me, and his nose is cold and wet and vaguely silky and it feels like the hide of a seal.

You didn't even give me a way home, I say, clenching my hands in the fur of his face. Curling my fingers around his teeth, pulling his jaw open. Even if I tried to go, you didn't even let me have a road. What the hell do I do with all this snow?

He tosses his head back. I have to look at him for a few minutes before I understand.

·························

Daddy, you drained the snowmobile. You broke through yourself, ran away, but you made yourself come back. You took away the roads, the light, but you made yourself come back. I don't know if you meant for Carol to die and I don't think it matters because either way I don't think I could ever forgive you. I don't know if you meant for Mama to die but I almost don't care anymore. Daddy, you've always been a bear, and you've always been too big for your skin, singing things you hated in the end, looking at children too small and weak to be yours. But bears can love, even if it's a love with teeth and claws, and even if you're a coward you're still something to ride.

Bears can't feel mercy. That's not what this is, and you can't fix anything. So carry me back down, Daddy, now that we're done. Take me back to the lights, back to heat and life, leave me there and be what you are. Be a bear. Let me not be.

Daddy's coat is warm and soft under my cheek. He bobs up and down as he walks, and it's like being rocked to sleep. I remember Carol in my arms, so warm and safe, and even more than that, I remember Daddy holding me, singing his growling bear-songs, trying to love me in the terrible way an animal can.

We never knew how to love each other, Daddy. Maybe someday we learn how to let each other go.

Carol is warm in his belly as he carries me—carries both of

us—toward the horizon. Toward what's left of the road. To our left the sun is inching up, giving us a little light for a few hours. It's precious. For the moment it's the three of us again, moving out of the night.

Daddy, we can't all be bears, and I have no fur to cover me. But there's a logic in why it's okay to leave at last. Death is so ugly and beauty is a lie, but the dawn is beautiful, and this is a lie I can tell myself for now.

.

I TELL THEE ALL, I CAN NO MORE

||||||||||||||||||||||||||||||||||||||||||||||||||||||||||||

HERE'S WHAT YOU'RE GOING TO DO. IT'S ALMOST LIKE A SCRIPT YOU
can follow. You don't have to think too much about it.

Just let it in. Let it watch you at night. Tell it everything it
wants to know. These are the things it wants, and you'll let it
have those things to keep it around. Hovering over your bed, all
sleek chrome and black angles that defer the gaze of radar. It's
a cultural amalgamation of one hundred years of surveillance.
There's safety in its vagueness. It resists definition. This is a huge
part of its power. This is a huge part of its appeal.

||||||||||||||||||||||||||

Fucking a drone isn't like what you'd think. It's warm. It probes,
gently. It knows where to touch me. I can lie back and let it do
its thing. It's only been one date but a drone isn't going to worry
about whether I'm an easy lay. A drone isn't tied to the conven-
tions of gendered sexual norms. A drone has no gender and, if it
comes down to it, no sex. Just because it can *do* it doesn't mean
it's a thing that it *has*.

We made a kind of conversation, before, at dinner. I did most
of the talking, which I expected.

The drone hums as it fucks me. We—the *dronesexual,* the
recently defined, though we only call ourselves this name to
ourselves and only ever with the deepest irony—we're never

43

sure whether the humming is pleasure or whether it's a form of transmission, but we also don't really care. We gave up caring what other people, people we probably won't ever meet, think of us. We talk about this on message boards, in the comments sections of blogs, in all the other places we congregate, though we don't usually meet face to face. There are no dronesexual support groups. We don't have conferences. There is no established discourse around who we are and what we do. No one writes about us but us, not yet.

The drones probably don't do any writing. But we know they talk.

Drones don't come, not as far as we can tell, but they must get satisfaction out of it. They must get something. I have a couple of orgasms, in the laziest kind of fashion, and the vibration of the maybe-transmission humming tugs me through them. I rub my hands all over that smooth conceptual hardware and croon.

||||||||||||||||||||||||||||

There was no singular point in time at which the drones started fucking us. We didn't plan it, and maybe it wasn't even a thing we consciously wanted until it started happening. Sometimes a supply creates a demand.

But when something is around that much, when it knows that much, it's hard to keep your mind from wandering in that direction. *I wonder what that would feel like inside me.* One kind of intimacy bleeds into another. Maybe the drones made the first move. Maybe we did. Either way, we were certainly receptive. *Receptive,* because no one penetrates drones. They fuck men and women with equal willingness, and the split between men and women in our little collectivity is, as far as anyone has ever been able to tell, roughly fifty-fifty. Some trans people, some gender-fluid, and all permutations of sexual preference represented by at least one or two members. The desire to fuck a drone seems to cross boundaries with wild abandon. Drones themselves are incredibly mobile and have never respected borders.

||||||||||||||||||||||||||||

Here's what you're going to do. You're not going to get too attached. This isn't something you'll have to work to keep from doing, because it's hard to attach to a drone. But on some level there is a kind of attachment, because the kind of closeness you experience with a drone isn't like anything else. It's not like a person. They come into you; they know you. You couldn't fight them off even if you wanted to. Which you never do. Not really.

||||||||||||||||||||||||||||

We fight, not because we have anything in particular to fight over, but because it sort of seems like the thing to do.

No one has ever come out and admitted to trying to have a relationship with the drone that's fucking them, but of course everyone knows it's happened. There are no success stories, which should say something in itself, and people who aren't in our circle will make faces and say things like *you can't have a relationship with a machine no matter how many times it makes you come* but a drone isn't a dildo. It's more than that.

So of course people have tried. How could you not?

This isn't a relationship, but the drone stayed the night after fucking me, humming in the air right over my bed as I slept, and it was there when I woke up. I asked it what it wanted and it drifted toward the kitchen, so I made us some eggs, which of course only I could eat.

It was something about the way it was looking at me. I just started yelling, throwing things.

Fighting with a drone is like fucking a drone in reverse. It's all me. The drone just dodges, occasionally catches projectiles at an angle that bounces them back at me, and this might amount to throwing. All drones carry two AGM-114 Hellfire missiles, neatly resized as needed, because all drones are collections of every assumption we've ever made about them, but a drone has never fired a missile at anyone they were fucking.

This is no-stakes fighting. I'm not even sure what I'm yelling about. After a while the drone drifts out the window. I cry and scream for it to call me. I order a pizza and spend the rest of the day in bed.

<hr />

Here's what you're going to do. You're not going to ask too many questions. You're just going to let it happen. You'll never know whose eyes are behind the blank no-eyes that see everything. There might not be any anymore; drones regularly display what we perceive as autonomy. In all our concepts of *droneness* there is hardly ever a human being on the other end. So there's really no one to direct the questions to.

Anyway, what the hell would you ask? *What are we doing, why are we this way?* Since when have those ever been answers you could get about this kind of thing?

<hr />

This is really sort of a problem. In that I'm focusing too much on a serial number and a specific heat signature that only my skin can know. In that I asked the thing to call me at all. I knew people tried things like this but it never occurred to me that it might happen without trying.

It does call me. I talk for a while. I say things I've never told anyone else. It's hard to hang up. That night while I'm trying to sleep I stare up at the ceiling and the dark space between me and it feels so empty.

I pass them out on the street, humming through the air. They avoid me with characteristic deftness but after a while it occurs to me that I'm steering myself into them, hoping to make contact. They all look the same but I know they aren't the same at all. I'm looking for that heat signature. I want to turn them over so I can find that serial number, nestled in between the twin missiles, over the drone dick that I've never actually seen.

Everyone around me might be a normal person who doesn't fuck a drone and doesn't want to and doesn't talk to them on the phone and usually doesn't take them to dinner. Or every one of them could be like that.

At some point we all stopped talking to each other.

Here's what you're going to do. Here's what you're not going to do. Here's a list to make it easy for you.

You're not going to spend the evening staring out the window. You're not going to toy endlessly with your phone. You're not going to masturbate furiously and not be able to come. You're not going to throw the things you threw at nothing at all. You're not going to stay up all night looking at images and video that you can only find on a few niche paysites. You're not going to wonder if you need to go back into therapy because you don't need therapy. You're not going to wonder if maybe you and people like you might be the most natural people in the entire world, given the way the world is now. You're not going to wonder if there was ever such a thing as *natural*.

Sometimes I wonder what it might be like to be a drone. This feels like a kind of blasphemy, and also pointless, but I do it anyway. So simple, so connected. So in tune. Needed instead of the one doing the needing. Possessing all the power. Subtly running more and more things until I run everything. The subjects of total organic surrender.

Bored, maybe, with all that everything. Playing some games.

It comes over. We fuck again and it's amazing. I'm almost crying by the end. It nestles against me and hums softer and I wonder how screwed I actually am in how many different ways.

Anyway, it stays the night again and we don't fight in the morning.

▨▨▨▨▨▨▨▨▨▨▨▨

A drone wedding. I want to punch myself in the mouth twenty or thirty times for even thinking that even for a second.

▨▨▨▨▨▨▨▨▨▨▨▨

It starts coming every night. This is something I know I shouldn't get used to but I know that I am. As I talk to it—before sex, during, after—I start to remember things that I'd totally forgotten. Things from my early childhood, things from high school that I didn't want to remember. I tell with tears running down my face and at the end of it I feel cleaned out and raw.

I don't want this to be over, I say. I have no idea what the drone wants and it doesn't tell me, but I want to believe that the fact that it keeps coming back means something.

I read the message boards and I wish I could tell someone else about this because I feel like I'm losing every shred of perspective. I want to talk about how maybe we've been coming at this from all the wrong angles. Maybe we should all start coming out. Maybe we should form political action groups and start demanding recognition and rights. I know these would all be met with utterly blank-screen silence but I want to say them anyway. I write a bunch of things that I never actually post, but I don't delete them either.

We're all like this. I'm absolutely sure that we're all like this and no one is talking about it but in all of our closets is a thing hovering, humming, sleek and black and chrome with its missiles aimed at nothing.

We have one more huge fight. Later I recognize this as a kind of self-defense. I'm screaming and beating at it with my fists, something about commitment that I'm not even sure that I believe, and it's just taking it, except for the moments when it butts me in the head to push me back. I'm shrieking about its missiles, demanding that it go ahead and vaporize my entire fucking apartment, put me out of my misery, because I can't take this anymore because I don't know what to do. We have angry sex and it leaves. It doesn't call me again. I stay in bed for two days and call a therapist.

Here's what you're going to do.

You're going to do what you told yourself you had the courage to do and say everything. You're going to let it all out to someone flesh and blood and you're going to hear what they say back to you. For once you're not going to be the one doing all the talking. You're going to be honest. You're going to be the one to start the whole wheel spinning back in the other direction. You're going to fix everything because you have the power to fix everything. You're going to give this all a name and say it like you're proud. You're going to bust open a whole new paradigm. You're going to be missile-proof and bold and amazing and you're not going to depend on the penetrative orgasmic power of something that never loved you anyway.

I stop at the door. I don't even make it into the waiting room.

I fiddle with the buttons on my coat. I check my phone for texts, voicemail. I look down the street at all those beautiful humming flying things. I feel a tug in the core of me where everything melts down into a hot lump and spins like a dynamo. I feel like I can't deny everything. I feel like I don't want to. I feel that the flesh is treacherous and doomed.

I made this promise to myself and it takes me half an hour on a bus and five minutes of staring at a name plaque and a glass door to realize that I don't want to keep it.

I look back out at everyone and I consider what it could be like to step through those doors, sit in a softly lit room with tissues and a lot of pastel and unthreatening paintings on the wall and spill it all and look up and see the therapist nodding, nodding knowingly, mouthing the words *me too*.

I don't really think anyone can help any of us.

Here's what you're going to do. You're going to stop worrying. You're going to stop asking questions. You're going to stop planning for tomorrow. You're going to go out and get laid and stop wondering what might have been. You're going to stop trying to fix anything. You're going to stop assuming there's anything to be fixed.

You're going to look out at all those drones and not wonder. You're going to look out at all those people and you're going to *know.* Even though no one is talking.

Me too. Me too. Me too.

ACROSS THE SEAM

||||||||||||||||||||||||||||||||||

So I might forget time, forget the world
My native land
My beloved land
I might find again, as in a blessed dream

—Petro Trokhanovskii, trans.

||||||||||||||||||||||||

It was not a battle because they were not aggressive,
nor were they defensive because they had no weapons
of any kind and were simply shot down like so many
worthless objects, each of the licensed life-takers
trying to outdo the others in butchery.

—Inscription on monument
erected at Lattimer, 1972.

LATTIMER, PENNSYLVANIA 1897

IN HIS DREAMS, BABA YAGA SETS FIRE TO THE SEAM AND DANCES with him as it burns.

This is the last thing she does, after the rest of the show she puts on for him—a show, she has always given him to understand, that she does not organize for his entertainment but hers. That first night, cold and alone and curled against a stoop with black dust choking his nostrils and coating his throat, without even yet the hard bed at the boarding house to make sleep a less terrible thing, she had come to him in her chicken-legged dacha, waving her spoon and laughing as if he was the funniest thing she had ever seen.

Well, look at this. All curled up like a cat—except no cat would ever put up with such cold. You're a long way from home, little dochka.

I'm not your daughter, he would have said, but one didn't argue with Baba Yaga, not even in dreams, unless one wanted to find oneself up to the neck in a soup pot. Instead he kept silent, then, and looked at the knobby chicken knees of her house and not at her crouching on her porch like a hunched black bird, pointing at him with her spoon.

The streets of the coal camp are muddy now and they were muddy then, only then the mud was half ice and somehow sucked and pulled even worse than when it was merely waterlogged. Men lost shoes. But the house of Baba Yaga seemed entirely unconcerned as it stood there.

But of course, it was a dream.

Don't you turn your gaze away from me, dochka. Don't sulk. I came a long way for you, and bad manners make a good supper.

55

Look up at me, curtsy, and pay me a proper thank-you when you meet my eyes.

It was as if the spoon had become a sword and pierced him through. She knew. Her eyes were like brittle knives when she laughed at him again. *Every part of her is sharp. Every part of her might carve, slice, alter.*

So now he looks forward to his dreams.

||||||||||||||||||||||||||||

Every day is much the same.

Out of bed before the sun; cold coffee and bread so dry it crumbles in his mouth. The boarding house smells like unwashed socks and stale drink, but he no longer notices it. He has been in the camp two weeks but his overalls are already worn as if he's had them for years and his boots badly need resoling. He covers his head with the hard shell of his helmet. He rubs the chin stubble that he's come to hate, but as yet he doesn't have enough company scrip to afford a good straight razor.

He is sixteen years old.

Iwan. Sometimes he's sure the shafts are whispering his name under the growls and coarse laughter of the other men. It began his first time down and he hasn't talked to anyone about it since then. Many days, he's sure that he's insane. When he sees the chicken-legged dacha in the center of the street. When the shafts speak to him. When he looks at the dresses of the boarding house's proprietress, her neatly coifed hair under her scarf, her hands—somehow both rough and delicate—and feels a yearning that has nothing to do with wanting her the way a man should want a woman.

He knows that he's broken.

Iwan, Baba Yaga murmurs to him as he staggers home under the weight of the coal dust and the low ceiling of the shaft, his back bent for so many hours that it is as though he carries the

weight of the entire mountain on his shoulders. *My little Iwanka.*
They don't know who you really are. Let us discuss what might
happen if they find out.

⁣ ⁣ ⁣ ⁣ ⁣ ⁣ ⁣ ⁣

The low mountains of western Pennsylvania are greening now,
coming out of a winter so brown and barren and long that he
had wondered if it might end at all. A few times there had been
snow—which at least was familiar—but there was much more
ice than snow, cold rain that leached into the bones and settled
there, and everywhere dead vegetation like the earth herself was
dying. At first, looking at the mine, seeing the dark scar of it and
the black hell inside, he had wondered if its poison was seeping
outward and infecting everything.

What have I come to, he had wondered then. *God.*

He no longer believes that God cares about him.

So now green life is creeping back into the mountains, but in
his dreams, perhaps to torture him, Baba Yaga sits him behind
her on her spoon and they fly across the ocean and back to the
rolling green hills of hory nashi—our mountains, dear and distant—and his heart aches as if it wants to burst from his chest
and bury itself in the soil of his birth.

You have to remember, Baba Yaga says, no mocking laughter
in her voice now, *where you came from. Such things can sustain*
you when nothing else does.

He shakes his head, in his dream, in his sleep, on his flat
boarding house pillow, his thin blanket gathered around his
shoulders. *I have nothing now. Not even this. Why are you*
showing this to me?

Baba Yaga does a little jig, more to prove a point than out of
any personal glee. She lowers her spoon and scoops up the earth,
pours it into his outstretched hands. It is nothing like the coal.
Iwanka, you are soft and deep like this here. And you can be hard

like the mountain into which you dig. You must be both in order to survive.

On the worst nights he dreams of the ship pulling into the harbor, the great statue lifting her torch over everything, the cold look in her eyes. Everyone else leaned over the deck and chattered, excited, and he thought of little birds flitting through his dense forests. She was welcoming to them, or they thought she was. But he looked up at her and he saw no welcome at all, and began to wonder if he had made a mistake.

The same coldness in the man with his many papers spread out in front of him.

Name? Place of origin? Are you literate? Where are you going? Is anyone meeting you there? He had stumbled through it in broken English, the little he had managed to scrape together in the passage. Iwan Charansky. Austria-Hungary. No. Lattimer.

No.

I am alone.

It was like confession. He hung his head and felt his cheeks burn.

The warmth of the stove in the early mornings. The lowing of the cattle, the soft jangle of their bells as he takes them to the fields. The sun rising over the mountains. Fresh paskha and pirohi with cheese. His father fixing prosfora and seed inside his pouch as he goes to plow the field, without which a good harvest will not be assured. Candlelit gilt and wood in the church, the knowing eyes of the saints in the ikonostas. Trying on his mother's best dress alone in the house, the terror of being caught. A scatter of grain in the sunlight like little beads of gold. Ice silvering the trees.

Screams. Fire—fire to consume a family that to others were always strangers, fire to consume the worrisome and the unwanted. Fire to consume the world.

Baba Yaga hands him this fire, like a fist, like a little burning heart in his cupped palms, and he understands that he has carried it with him from the green hills and across the ocean, and it is part of him now.

The seam, dochka. Give it to the seam.

This place is almost ready to burn.

Nights in the boarding house are becoming more interesting. Louder, more people, squeezing together in Big Mary's kitchen, listening to her talk. Sometimes he stands in the doorway and listens too. What's done to them. What might be done. Mary is offering fragments of another world, holes through which to glimpse it, like gold nestled in the coal. Something he has never imagined, let alone seen. Big Mary offers exhortations to the promise of America, to the rights of men, and the men nod and bang their mugs on the table and cry agreement. Some. Others sit silently, their arms folded, and he can tell that they have yet to be convinced. But they're listening.

Behind him, he can feel Baba Yaga folding the spindles of her fingers and grinning. She whispers, *This is also my dochka. She knows me, even if she doesn't call me by name. Look at her: wouldn't she make a tasty stew? But her spirit is too big for my pot, and I have other uses for her. She is also carrying the fire. My fire.*

You should watch her. You are sisters, you and she. Even if she can never know.

More and more, Baba Yaga is coming to him in his waking hours.

This should perhaps frighten him more than it does.

Every night, now, the seam burns. The whole mountain runs with flame like a river. He watches it, and it seems to him that there are figures in the flames, bright and beautiful. They are not in pain. They are dancing, and they are holding out arms of cinder and glowing coal and beckoning to him to dance with them.

His mother is there. His father. Their faces are alight with pride as they behold their only son. Only now they see him for what he truly is, and there is no blame and no shame and not a hint of rejection. They love him as he is. *Iwanka,* his mother sings, her fingers like sparks as she whirls through the dying trees. *I have a lovely little dress for you, and look, I made for you this scarf. Look how bright it is.*

If anyone touches you after this, to harm you, they will burn, and not with us.

He wakes up with tears scalding his cheeks. They smoke and steam.

Goddamn hunkies.

When at last he has enough scrip saved to buy a razor, the man in the company store overcharges him. He expects it, would have even borne it as yet another in a long line of harsh treatments, except that the amount the man is demanding is more than he has. He's been borrowing a razor from one of the other men in the boarding house, but it's too blunt and it hurts him, and the shave it gives is nowhere clean enough. It's a small thing, and he doesn't even know why it should be so important to him, except that he does.

Baba Yaga is teaching him to face hard truths. He's not the quickest of learners when it comes to things like that but he does learn.

Goddamn hunkies, the man growls when Iwan tries, stuttering through the words, to explain, to try to convince the man to take what he has as sufficient for the blade. *You come here, think you don't have to speak the language, think you're special. Owed special treatment. You won't get it from me, you little rat. Give me the price of it or get the hell out of the store.*

But it *is* special treatment. It always has been. *Hunky. Polack. Little rat.* For a long time now he's been used to it, but Big Mary is suggesting that he shouldn't be, that he's more than just some hunky rat crawling on his belly through the shafts. And there's Baba Yaga, folding all the hunky rats into her arms, her hands black with the coal, giving them firesides and warm porridge with milk, chalky with powdered bones.

There is something else that his saved scrip will buy. He stares at it for some long minutes the next time he goes to the company store to buy what little food he can. He stares at it for as long as he can, for as long as he thinks is safe, before he's noticed. A pair of lady's gloves, white and soft, very plain and, he knows, not fine. It seems strange to find them in a store that only stocks the necessities of the working people of Lattimer, but there they are, and to his weary eyes they seem to shine as if they were made of ivory. They are free of coal dust, pure, like the polished bones of someone long-dead. Of the stuff that Baba Yaga grinds for her porridge.

Strange things are beautiful to him now.

He wants to buy them. He wants them more than the razor. He imagines sliding his hands into them, the hair on his knuckles and the callouses on his palms and the black dust packed under his fingernails hidden by that elegant white. They would make his fingers look slender, he knows. Delicate. Before he turns away he reaches out and runs a fingertip along their backs.

Hey, hunky. He pulls his hand back as if he's been burned; his face *is* burning, his neck and ears, and he's praying that the big man behind the counter won't see. *Buy something or get out. You here to browse like a fucking woman?*

Take me back to hory nashi, he whispers to Baba Yaga as he slinks out of the place, feeling her heat and her glee at his side. In the shadows of the town he could swear he sees a *dacha* shuffling, out of the way like any other house but for its legs. *Take me back there and bury me in the ground with the ashes of my family.*

No, dochka, she laughs. *Better for you, given that you're mine. The things you want will be yours. They will have to be.*

<hr>

She tells him stories about ordeals, in the shafts, in the lukewarm water he uses for his quick baths, in the doorway of the boarding house kitchen. She tells him stories of walking on hot coals to prove one's innocence, of burning women as witches and trusting to God to care for their souls if they proved free of the influence of the devil. *They were all my daughters, Iwanka. They danced with me in the moonlight and the fire, as you do.*

I'm not a witch, he insists. But he lifts his blackened hands and, as if they are someone else's, his own fingers trace ancient symbols across his arms, his face. He smears it over his lips, turning them dark and full. Baba Yaga nods in approval.

Not a witch, no, maybe. But were they *witches? I tell you truly, dochka, there have always been those of us who simply didn't fit, and those ones tend to be of a kind. And you are my sweet little daughter, and you will never be one of them. The others.*

Why would you want to be?

She places his burning hands against the seam and Lattimer fails its test in an orgy of flame.

<hr>

It comes in the fall, with the rain and the cold wind. The trees are aflame, red and gold, and as the strike is called, as the marches begin, he marches with them but his gaze is locked on those burning branches, each one like the embodiment of God sent to give him a message. Big Mary cries out to them, her arms lifted, praising them as if they are her children and newly learned to stand on their own. There is word that the company will shortly send in the strike-breakers, but there is fearlessness on the sharp wind, at least for the moment, and they tell each other to be strong. Even him, no longer just a hunky rat but, for a short and precious time, a brother among brothers.

He accepts this with certain reservations. Baba Yaga leads the march in her chicken-legged dacha, standing on the porch and waving her spoon like a general.

What would his mother think of this? His father? If their spirits could travel from dust to dust, emerge from the mountain and see him now? Would they be proud? Would any of this surprise them? Their lost son, marching with the lost and demanding to be found again?

Still more lost than any of them, though they can't see it now? Does he still care?

<hr>

Yet the actual moment, when it comes, isn't in the rain or the cold wind but on a warm, sunny day in early September that still contains hints of dying summer, the last of the green before the fire begins to turn it to gray ash. It's a big march—nearly three hundred of them, or so the rumor goes—and there is such a sense of quiet strength among them all that even Baba Yaga ceases her cackling, though he senses that this is not out of any particular respect so much as it is that she is waiting. That the world around them is holding its breath.

That the ground is heating under their feet.

There are fires far below, Baba Yaga whispered once, *that have burned for hundreds of years. Longer. There is a single great fire beneath it all that has been burning since the birth of the world.*

When the sheriff issues the call to disperse, Iwan barely hears it. It's a voice far removed, present but ultimately not very important, and at any rate no one is dispersing. From somewhere far away there's a scuffle, the sound of feet scrabbling and the grunt of bodies hitting bodies, but this, too, seems unimportant. Everyone around him is standing, standing like stones.

Then. "Give two or three shots!"

Now a murmur. Now people turning to each other, alarmed, the quiet strength drifting away like ash. And as the shots ring out, he looks to Baba Yaga and sees her grin eating up her face. *Grandmother Chaos,* he thinks. *Grandmother Fire.* And the people scatter into madness.

It's the spark. He can feel it. It warms him as he runs with the crowd down the muddy streets, as more shots and screams ring out, pain and anger, the sound of fighting. He looks behind and sees fallen bodies, clothes streaked with blood; he turns away again and keeps running.

He has always been running, since he was set into motion. Now it ends.

It comes to him that Baba Yaga has left the porch of her dacha and is on his back, riding him, beating him with her spoon like a horse. He goes where she points him, breaking away from the fleeing crowd, and isn't surprised to find himself standing in front of the shop. Baba Yaga leaps up on his shoulders and shatters the glass of the front window with her spoon.

The razor. The gloves. In a few seconds he has them, though now his arms are bleeding from stray shards. It feels like fair trade. If trade was even necessary; perhaps these things are his, his from the very birth of the world, like magical things waiting for him in a dragon's cave.

And to the dragon's cave she is now driving him.

He runs past the fleeing bodies in the streets, running against the flow. No one notices him or the things in his hands. Once he thinks he hears the cry of Big Mary rising over the shots and screams, and when he turns at the bottom of a little hill he sees her standing there above him, her arms raised and tears streaming down her face. She's muddy, dirty, but somehow she is shining in the sun like a piece of cut anthracite. Their gazes meet and he knows that she sees him, and that she sees him for what he is. Their fundamental kinship.

In this moment he has her blessing.

Give it to the seam.

He turns and runs again, and the shaft opens up like a mouth and swallows him.

———

It is so very much like a story. Baba Yaga has drawn him into it, him and his true self that waits for him in the shadows. She has spun it around herself like a cloak, from coal seams and fairy gold. This is his journey, from the green hills and forested mountains of his homeland to the coal and the black and the fire, and for once he feels that it is exactly as it should be.

And here in the glittering dark anything might be possible.

The line between truth and story is so thin, Baba Yaga whispers. *Here, thinner still. You are a child of the story, dochka, half in and half out of the world. No one will tell your tale, but I will keep you safe and tell it to myself within the walls of my house; I will feed it to my oven and bake it in my black bread.*

Now give the fire to the seam and dance with me in the ashes.

Iwan, Iwanka, Janus-faced and true to herself at last, presses her hands against the coal and finds a hard stone that holds a spark within its cold heart. She lifts the razor and strikes, and gives what lies inside to the seam that has run through her life and her world. She turns them both to ash and dust.

———

Wagons carry the dead into the lands beyond like fallen heroes. There are cries for vengeance. There are ordeals that are failed and others that are passed, there is condemnation and a trial, and in the end there is memory of a kind, though no one tells the story of Iwan-who-was-not-Iwan and who was no fool, and how he vanished into the dark after death came to Lattimer.

But there is fire. There is fire that burns forever in that dark, and in the flames Iwanka dances with Baba Yaga and eats her black bread and her porridge of powdered bone and sweet milk. She dances in the arms of her parents and the other dead, and she dances all the way back to hory nashi, to the green and the trees, to the older fires and the memory that sits in the stones like glowing coals. She is with the scattered ones, even the ones who have been forgotten, and the great secret that Baba Yaga sings to those who can hear is that even they have a way of living forever, until, like wheat, they emerge from rich earth, green and new and reaching their arms toward a clear sky.

DISPATCHES FROM A HOLE IN THE WORLD

||||||||||||||||||||||||||||||||||||||||||||||||||||||||||||||||||||||||||||

I'M STANDING IN THE ELEVATOR. THE ELEVATOR ISN'T MOVING.
Neither am I. It seems, for the moment, like simply staring at
what's in front of me is the simplest and therefore the best immediate project. Far simpler than the dissertation that's supposed
to start here.

But I can't avoid it forever.

I'm not sure what I expected, but the place is small. It's tucked
into three floors of a generic office building a few blocks from
the Library of Congress. From the outside it doesn't look like
much of anything; they probably wanted it like that. But what
I'm specifically staring at is what looks like the floor of a college library, one of those more industrial ones unconcerned with
any popularly conceived aesthetic of Libraryness. White walls,
recessed lighting, long desks divided into little cubicles, each
equipped with a small, slim computer terminal.

It's empty.

I take a breath, and I step out of the elevator and into an
archive of three hundred thousand and seventy-six recorded
suicides.

|||||||||||||||||||||||||||

When it happened it was like a plague.

No one was sure how it was spreading, or why, or who was

going to be next. People feared for their loved ones, their friends and family. People feared for themselves. Pundits proclaimed doom with excited solemnity. Religious leaders got gleeful hard-ons for apocalypse. People blamed technology, peer pressure, the alienation of a generation raised in the midst of crushing debt and recession and increasingly extreme weather and constant war and a general sense of hopelessness.

You know, kids today.

But when that nightmare year was over and things finally began to taper off, all we were left with was questions.

Everyone had at least a tenuous connection with someone who died. That's what happens now—you know people who know people who know people, you follow people without ever actually speaking to them but you communicate in likes and retweets and reblogs. I've had entire friendships that were based around reposting the same series of makeup tutorials. The same collections of gifsets. So suddenly you're watching them die. It scrolls past on your feed, on your dash. It felt like an attack. For a while people thought it was an attack. Yet another one, dudebros against the Social Justice Whatevers.

But that wasn't what was going on.

So we watched. Some of us looked away. Some of us said they vomited, said they experienced panic attacks that lasted for hours. It's very hard to explain what it was like for us, because we were there in a way our parents weren't, and in a way our kids won't be. You live through a terrorist attack, you live in it, you're one of the shell-shocked survivors huddled in blankets, you're brushing ashes and bone-dust out of your hair. Smoke in your eyes.

We survived. We moved on, to the extent you ever can. Those of us academically inclined—who could find places in the decaying zombie corpse of academia—we did what we do. We over-analyze. So we wrote about it. Term papers. Research papers, self-reflective essays. Short stories, poems—for a while there the MFA programs got really morbid. We work out our demons however we can. We splash our trauma all over everything.

But as far as I know, I'm the only one to ever take it this far. Because it means going back. Living it. All over again.

My estimated time to completion for this project is two years.

Two years in the Year of Suicide.

⁘⁘⁘⁘⁘⁘⁘⁘⁘⁘⁘

It's a Vine, from back when Vine was still a thing. Dude put his phone down on a stand or propped it up some other way. He's sitting in a blue beanbag chair. He's white, dark-haired, maybe about fourteen. The room looks like your standard middle-class teenage boy's room. If I looked at the dossier file all the pertinent information would be there, at least what could be collected without special permission from the family—which some gave and some didn't.

I'm not going to look at the file, because that's not how I saw it. I didn't even know it was coming. If I had my way I'd be looking at this in the dark at three in the morning with cold pizza and a bong.

But I'm here. Watching this looping six seconds.

The boy is looking straight at the camera. He has no discernable expression. He lifts one hand; he holds a kitchen knife. He holds it to his throat and slashes his carotid artery. Blood jets to the side and gushes down his shirt. He slumps. Hand twitches and falls.

Repeat.

This boy takes six seconds to die. He dies over and over.

As far as anyone has been able to determine, this is Patient Zero.

⁘⁘⁘⁘⁘⁘⁘⁘⁘⁘⁘

When I was thirteen I read about Jonestown.

I was a morbid kid to begin with. I hated violence, actually—I was disturbed by gory TV and movies until I was almost in my twenties. Covered my eyes for the chest-burster scene in Alien. I was revolted by torture porn horror. I couldn't handle watching animals in pain.

But I was fascinated by history, and the history of murder on massive scales.

So I read about Auschwitz. I read about Hiroshima. I devoured books on the Rwandan genocide. I was fascinated by the gruesomeness of it all, but even more I think I was fascinated by the extremity. What drives people to do things like this? What drives people to slaughter each other?

What drives people to slaughter themselves?

Jonestown was the worst. Because at least according to my understanding at the time, those people did it to themselves. I read about it and I imagined myself there in the pavilion with the rest of them, waiting in line for poison, watching people going into convulsions. I imagined watching mothers feeding it to their babies with syringes. I imagined what it would have been like after, sitting there and looking at the empty cup of your death, waiting to feel it and knowing there was nothing you could do. All those people—afraid, not afraid, just...in those moments of pre-oblivion.

I imagined those moments as either utterly insane or marked by the most profound sanity a human being can experience. Except that's wrong. Insanity isn't so clear-cut. It isn't so simple. Neither is suicide. What suicide means. It's abhorrent to do that to a complex idea. To a lived fact.

We understand that a lot better than we did.

But that pavilion. Nine hundred and thirteen people. Those aerial photographs. I stared at them. For a long time.

I thought, I am looking at a hole in the world.

Then the Year. Three hundred thousand and seventy-six holes

in the world, opening up one after the other after the other, like bullet holes, like mouths, like eyes.

Except that number isn't reliable. Those are only the ones we know about.

Those are only the ones we saw.

⸻

The next one is a girl. Mid-teens, Hispanic, very pretty. Standing on a chair, rope around her neck. It appears to be nighttime; the lights in her bedroom are on. Stuffed animals just visible on the bed. Makeup scattered across the dresser like she was in the middle of messing with some eyeshadow when the idea occurred to her. She lifts her phone, stares expressionlessly into it as she adjusts the angle. The phone jerks. It's clear that she kicked the chair away. The phone swings wildly and falls. You see a shot of her feet swinging. Then it cuts off.

This one went up on YouTube. Within a couple of hours it had over twenty thousand views. You know how they say don't read the comments? Oh my God, do not read the fucking comments.

Those were archived along with the video. They're part of the historical record.

I watch it a couple of dozen times through, and halfway into those couple of dozen times I start going frame by frame, making notes. Of everything I can see. Of what I'm feeling. Part of the point of this project is self-reflexivity. I'll code later. For now I just need to get down everything I can.

⸻

About a month into the Year people started asking a very obvious question. Not why, and not how, and not how in the hell is this spreading like a virus—and that was pretty hilarious. Whole new meaning to the term viral.

Everyone who documented their own deaths…They died. They were dead. Some of them could set things to share automatically and some of them appeared to have done so, but others…

Who the fuck was uploading these things?

Like I said. In the end all we had were questions.

Older girl, early twenties, black. Blank-faced. Messy college dorm room. Bottle of pills. She empties them into her mouth gulp by gulp and washes them down with vodka. This one goes on for a while. When she drops to the floor, she manages to prop her phone up where we can see at least part of her. Her face.

This one isn't gory, but it's one of the uglier ones I watch.

Five times, notes, then I need to quit for the night.

I expect to have nightmares. I'm ready for it. I wake up shivering and too hot and I spend a feverish few minutes on my phone, recording my thick, roaring dreams. I manage to fall back asleep. It takes a while. In the morning I save what I wrote for all that coding I intend to do later.

The archive was very controversial when it was first proposed, and the controversy hasn't disappeared. A lot of people would just as soon forget that year.

A lot of those people were parents. Adults. People protested, made petitions. But us…Even those of us who carried around all our mental scar tissue, stiff and raw, we didn't want to let go. Even if we couldn't look at it, couldn't watch, couldn't even think about it without fight-or-flight chemicals flooding into our blood, we wanted to keep it. The record of our Year.

A lot of it is that this is what we do. We document. We display. It was real. It's ours.

But a lot of it is that, even if we didn't and still don't understand why, those people—our people—wanted to be seen. Wanted those final moments to be out there. Maybe they weren't thinking straight, maybe they were just crazy, maybe something else was going on. Fuck, maybe it was demon possession. But they wanted it.

Pics or it didn't happen. Didn't they used to say that? Maybe it was horrifying. Sure.

But it was ours.

⫿⫿⫿⫿⫿⫿⫿⫿⫿⫿⫿⫿⫿⫿⫿⫿

Ages of the victims range from ten to twenty-five, most of them on the lower end. There was something about puberty, went the theory, but of course no one ever verified that in any way aside from what people observed. People noted—repeatedly—the suspicious roundness of those numbers, but no one ever based any concrete conclusions on that either.

For a while people were talking about a particular kind of parasite that infects the brains of insects and drives them to kill themselves. A specific kind of fungus that affects the behavior of ants in bizarre ways and then sprouts from the head, grows and releases spores. They did autopsies, and they found nothing.

They found no drugs. No unusual substances.

Some of the people who died had been exhibiting signs of depression and/or anxiety, sure. A fair number had difficult home lives. Plenty of them were queer, and a lot of those weren't out to anyone but their friends online.

Of course they were going through that shit. They were kids. We were kids, and being a kid is hell, and adults forget that.

We didn't want to forget.

⁂

I spend most of the next day going through more of it. Gifs, Vines, videos uploaded to various places. Still images, selfies; Instagram. Screenshots of Snapchats. Sometimes there's sound and sometimes there isn't, but the common thread running through it all is imagery.

Another couple of clips of people cutting their own throats. I remember hanging being popular. A few people tying plastic bags over their heads. One especially industrious boy douses himself in gasoline in his driveway and lights a match.

I wander outside to eat and get a tasteless hot dog at a lunch truck. I feel dazed. The color seems to be bleeding out of the world.

I have two years of this to go.

⁂

I spend the rest of the week on a proposal for a dissertation grant I don't expect to be awarded. This thing is too weird. It's too disturbing. I don't think the NSF is going to want to touch it with a thirty-foot pole. But I need the money, and I badly need something else to focus on.

⁂

I wasn't going to read the dossiers carefully until I finished preliminary data collection, but a couple of weeks later I start going through them. I expect it to afford me some distance, but it doesn't. Maybe the information is dry and clinical, but one of the things that makes me good at this is an ability to con- sume dry, clinical information and translate it into something vital and real and immediate. Something bloody. I sit there in my carrel on the third floor with a pile of printouts—I wanted to work with paper for this, and in here I have to—and I make notes until my eyes hurt, and then I sit back and close them and think about how scared we were and how all we felt like we had was each other, except we didn't know which one of us was going to be next.

I used to wonder if, when my brain started trying to kill me, I would know what was happening.

When I open my eyes it's almost midnight and the woman from the front desk is shaking me. They need to close up. I need to go home.

I don't go home. I wander around downtown until dawn. I look at the Capitol dome and I think about how none of those people in there have anything to do with us. About how, after the Year of Suicide, we all gave up. Voting rates for our generation are the lowest of any generation in history. They bemoan this, our apathy. How disappointing it is. How disappointing we all are.

Look: don't you judge us for opting out of a fucking lie. Don't you ever do that.

We went to war and a lot of us didn't come home, and none of you ever noticed.

I get the grant.

In the end the thing that allowed the archive to exist was the decision that it would have no connection to any outside network.

None. Security is unbelievably tight. We can't bring in phones. We can't bring in any kind of recording device whatsoever. We can bring in paper and pens and pencils and highlighters, and we can make printouts of text. No images. That's it.

It's like the Hot Zone of social media. Because that's what it is, isn't it? It's a giant data quarantine.

They scrubbed the net as clean as they could. They sent in people to confiscate hard drives of all sizes. We're pretty sure they got it all. Once the archive was established, a lot of us voluntarily turned over what we had and deleted everything else. We organized around it. We surprised people, and we baffled people. They didn't understand.

Well, whatever. They don't need to.

The situation is less than ideal, but that was true from the beginning. That was true before the Year. That's always been true.

⁙⁙⁙⁙⁙⁙⁙⁙⁙⁙⁙⁙⁙

I go out to dinner with some friends from my program, and as I'm texting them from the restaurant where I've arrived early, I realize that it's my favorite sushi place and I haven't been here in five months, and these are the only remaining friends I ever see face to face and I haven't seen any of them in almost as long.

And I realize I'm only now realizing that, and I think Huh.

It's a vague kind of dinner, and that's mostly on my end. They talk about work, about the projects they've hooked up with, about their own dissertations. Kayla has a gig at a marketing firm, which is going well. Mike also got that grant I was awarded and we high five.

All these common things that tied us together since the first year in the program are still there, but as the evening proceeds it becomes apparent that there are new things in which I don't and can't share. Mike got that grant; Mike and his husband are also about to adopt a baby. Lissa is getting married in a couple of months and the planning for that is in full swing. With her spot at the firm, Kayla is thinking she might be able to get a down payment on a house in the not-too-distant-future.

And I'm just listening.

So what have you been up to? What you got going on?

Well, after this I'm probably going to go back to my basement apartment and leaf through a binder full of notes I took while I watched fifty-five kids aged thirteen through nineteen erase their faces with shotguns.

So I got that going on.

Sitting there, staring down at my tuna rolls, I feel like darkness is creeping across the table and it's carving me apart from them. Once we used to go out and drink until we were practically falling down, to ease the pain of endless unendurable lectures. We were united by cheerful misery, and there was something wonderful about that union. It felt full and alive.

They moved on. They moved forward. They have lives. But every time I touch this thing I'm getting dragged backward.

And I'm not so sure about alive anymore.

<hr />

Kayla calls me the next morning. I have an incredible hangover. Not the worst in a while, though, and not from dinner. I came home after, I leafed through the binder, and I drank until I passed out on top of it.

I just want to make sure you're okay.

Sure, I'm okay. Why wouldn't I be okay?

You seemed kind of. She doesn't finish that sentence, and I can't tell if it's because she doesn't want to or she doesn't know how. I dunno, I just. We hadn't heard from you in a while, and I just wanted to check in.

Check in. Fuck's sake, I'm fine. She's not my mother, I have a mother. I haven't spoken to her in about three weeks, but I still have one.

Kayla's voice drops. Look, you know...You have this thing, and everyone thinks it's kind of...Just don't disappear, okay? You remember. You remember what it was like.

Suddenly she sounds so gentle, and my throat closes up, and I remember the one time she and I got so drunk and so comfortable with each other that a week after meeting for the first time we were sitting in a bar yelling to each other about our worst sexual experiences practically at the top of our lungs.

That was a little over six years after the Year. We were healing but we were all still hurting. We needed each other.

Yes, Kayla, I remember.

Do you?

I have stacks of binders and I have stacks of highlighters and I have stacks of pens and I have no idea what to do with any of them anymore. I work all the time, but then I stop working and I stare at it and I think, What exactly is all this? Who left it here? Who would do this?

Why?

I have a year left.

My grant runs out.

It didn't take us very long to stop looking for answers.

Other people, people outside the trenches—sure, they kept looking. They were desperate. They never stopped looking until things began to taper off and then even after. For a while. Then they did stop. No one officially called off the search. They just…stopped.

But we stopped long before that.

Because the why didn't matter. We didn't have the luxury of why. We didn't have the time or the effort to expend on why. I'm not saying we didn't wonder. Everyone wondered. But after the initial flood of panic, after it became clear that it wasn't stopping, that it was only getting worse, we turned inward and we did what no one else seemed able to do.

We took care of each other.

We stayed in contact. We formed networks of information-sharing and retooled existing ones, and we pooled our resources. We sent people to homes, to sit with and comfort and be with people who were lonely and scared. We helped people in bad situations get out of them. We raised money. We ran seminars and workshops. We got medication to people who needed it. We did highly organized damage control.

We were doing all that before the Year even happened. All the Year did was kick it into high gear.

There did come a point—and it didn't take, thank Christ—where they were talking seriously about going to the sources and shutting everything down. Taking it all away from us.

The death toll was already horrifying. Believe me when I tell you: You don't even want to think about what it might have been.

||||||||||||||||||||||||||||

Sitting with my binders and my highlighters and my pencils and my pens in the dark, looking at my phone on the coffee table. Little screen blinks on. Buzz. Blinks off. Green-purple rectangle, floating in the air in front of me like a ghost.

Blinks on. Buzz. Blinks off.

It's just an alarm. I haven't actually spoken to anyone, in any sense of the term, in over a week.

All these binders full of the dead. All these binders of me in and among and with them. So what does that make me?

***

Here's how it was: We were dying. But we weren't alone.

Suddenly we all knew each other. Suddenly we were all friends. We were all family. Across media and networks and apps and sites and everything you can think of. Sure, some things got seriously ugly, but by the time it became clear what we were dealing with, for the most part people laid down their arms. Truces and ceasefires were declared. We had bigger things to worry about.

We were dying.

I loved those people. I loved every one of them. The people I never met. The people whose names and faces I never knew until I was watching them kill themselves. The people who mourned for them and invited me to mourn with them. We said we loved each other. We all said it. Over and over. Like hands across a chasm, groping in the dark. Knowing that, in the end, we probably couldn't save anyone. All we could do was be there until they were gone, and be with whoever was left.

I remember how it was. I remember it. I remember it so well. I'm drowning in remembering.

Not very shareable.

I love you. I love you.

I love you.

***

After it was over, I was lonelier than I had ever been in my entire life.

My notes are in chaos. My coding is an incoherent mess. None of it makes any sense at all, and I'm not sure it ever did. I have no idea how to organize this into something that could even begin to vaguely resemble something defensible.

I have six months. But that time-to-completion was just an estimate. My advisor is very hands-off. No one is holding me to that deadline but me.

In theory, I suppose, I could just stay here.

So there I am.

I don't know how long I stare at it. I know my back starts to hurt and my mouth is dry, and my eyes itch and my head aches, but I'm pretty sure that was all already the case. I sit under those college-library overhead lights and I stare at the screen and it doesn't matter how long I do that because it doesn't change and it isn't going to.

The little clock in the corner of the screen says ten minutes to midnight. I think maybe it's said that for a while.

There I am.

It's a grainy selfie. Poorly lit. It's been put through a filter which has done it no favors. The colors are all fucked and it's hard to make out anything clearly, but I can see enough.

I'm sitting on the floor in front of the coffee table. I can't see the coffee table but I know it's there, just beyond where the phone is. I'm staring into the camera. I have no discernable expression.

I'm not holding the phone.

We want to wrap things up neatly. We want to come out the other side and look back and be able to make sense of it all. We want to beat fear and pain and loss into narrative submission; this explains the persistence of war stories, and the persistence of their telling.

We record, we write our histories, we analyze and we theorize, we editorialize, we engage in punditry. We publish. We curate and we archive. We do this because we have to, because we can't just leave it all there. We can't just look down at that endless mass of corpses and let that be the last word.

We can't leave the holes in the world.

I wish I could tell you something. I wish I could give you an answer. But in the end no answer could have made any difference. And the questions we were left with never mattered.

All we ever had was each other.

EVENT HORIZON

||||||||||||||||||||||||||||||

ON TUESDAYS AND THURSDAYS WE GO TO FEED THE HOUSE.

Zhan takes me. We walk down the cracked sidewalk, hopping the places where the cracks are almost chasms. At points we have to push through high weeds. We go in the middle of the day when the sun is a hammer beating on your head and it's too hot for the flies to buzz. There's hardly anyone outside then and never anyone down this end of Pine Street, which is probably the only reason we can come and feed the house at all.

Because if the rest of them had their way they'd just let it starve.

Can you starve a house? I asked Zhan once, and he just spat tobacco at me and smirked. It was a stupid question and I know that now. Of course you can starve a house. You can starve anything that's alive.

Zhan flips his shaggy black hair back from his face, huffs out a laugh at nothing in particular. Zhan is three years older than me and all angles and he doesn't know I'm in love with him.

In my mind, all three of those things are of equal importance. In my mind, none of them can exist independently of the others.

Zhan has two squirrels in a steel box trap under his arm. They scurry back and forth and rattle the wire mesh on the ends. I can feel their panic. Once it would have bothered me but I'm over that now. I'm focused ahead, trying not to trip over anything but also because I want to see the house the second that seeing it is possible. I don't want it sneaking up on me. It keeps up the appearance of dormancy but we know that it's like any predator; it only seems passive when it has to.

"Step it up, Tom." Zhan glances back over his shoulder and speeds up a little. We're not supposed to be here. If we're seen by an adult nosy enough we'll get busted for truancy and they'd probably want to know what we were going to do with the squirrels. I move faster, grass whispering around my ankles.

Then I see it.

It's two stories. There's a porch running around its front and a little way onto the sides. Its blue paint has faded and peeled until it's almost gray. Its front yard is dead and brown. The four front windows—two on each floor—are broken. They're black holes. We've never seen what's inside. We've never gotten close enough to do so. A rusty PRIVATE PROPERTY KEEP OUT sign hangs crooked on the wire mesh fence but that's not why we hang back.

Zhan and I stand there for a few minutes. The squirrels are still and silent, and I know without looking that it isn't because they're afraid. They're beyond fear.

Finally Zhan drops into a crouch and sets down the trap, points the front at the gap where the gate used to be before it rusted off its hinges. He opens the trap. I lose the fight against the shiver that wants to roll through me; there's sweat trickling down between my shoulder blades, but that's not where the shiver is coming from.

The house is staring at me. At both of us.

The squirrels walk out of the trap. They aren't moving in that funny little hop that squirrels do. They're *walking*, one foot in front of the other, stiff. They're little squirrel zombies. They walk through the gate without hesitation, up the broken pavement of the front path and right up to the door.

Here's the thing about the door: It's there. And it's not.

They walk right up to it and through it. It never opens.

No sound. No movement.

"Every fuckin' time," Zhan murmurs. I nod.

Zhan picks up the trap. We back away. Twenty yards clear and we turn and walk back the way we came. Neither of us says a word.

‖‖‖‖‖‖‖‖‖‖‖‖‖‖‖‖‖‖‖‖

The house has always been there. Or it was there when we moved here, which was before I can remember anything, so as far as I'm concerned that's *always*.

Zhan and I have been friends since I was old enough to have friends and he's been my hero since I was old enough to have heroes. A lot of this is because he accepted me from the first when a lot of other kids laughed and called names and threw rocks and never gave me a moment's peace at school—most particularly the ever-present trio of Kyle Patterson, who has hated me for reasons of his own since the third grade, Jake McDonnell, who's his best friend, and Drew Carter, who usually just tags along because he has nothing better to do—because of my hair and the clothes I insisted on wearing and how I bristled every time anyone called me *her*. I could never have explained to them why I wanted these things; they just felt right in a world that was nothing but wrong. But Zhan, if he didn't understand, at least accepted without question or complaint. For Zhan, I just was. I am.

Like the house.

I was ten when Zhan first took me to the house. He had caught a neighbor's cat, a mangy thing that always came after us with claws fully extended. It hissed and yowled in the trap but then it walked through the front gate and we never saw it again.

Zhan swore me to secrecy. I swore.

That was three years ago. In those three years Zhan has never answered any of my questions, not where it came from, what it really is, how he found out about it, or whether or not we could kill it. I think if there were answers, Zhan would give them to me.

Later in the woods, after we've fed the house, he sticks a hot dog into fire we made in a ring of stones and holds it out to me when it's split down the middle and steaming. The light is touching his face with soft, shifting fingers. I look at him and I hope—oh, God, I *hope*—that he can't see what I'm thinking.

I knew I was in love with Zhan a year after he showed me the house. I think the house is why it happened. He shared a secret with me. It made me want to share all of mine.

||||||||||||||||||||||||||||||

It's getting tough to do the twice-a-week-sneaking-out thing.

Back in summer it was easier. We could get away for entire days, spend the morning tossing a baseball back and forth in the dusty lot two blocks from our street, check the traps, feed the house, and devote the rest of the afternoon to shooting crows with an air rifle from the bushes that surround the parking lot of the Los Vientos industrial park. In the summer it's pretty empty so no one runs us off. But I think Zhan always enjoys that part more than I do.

Regardless, it's not summer anymore. School's back in session, never mind how hot it is and will be for at least two more months, and it's not all that hard to go truant from lunch with all of us crowded into the blacktop yard—*blasting* heat at us—but we're running a little bit of a risk every time.

Thank Christ no one really cares. *That fucking dyke and her faggot friend.* Neither of us is especially popular, so okay, we have each other.

We have each other. I love how that sounds.

Here we are again. This time it's three chipmunks, walking in stately procession up the path. Zhan and I are standing close enough to touch. I glance at him—it always feels hard to look away from the house, dangerous even, but I can manage it for him—and for the first time I wonder *How much longer are we going to do this?*

What would happen if we stopped?

I don't know why Zhan started feeding the house. But in bed that night I start thinking about that steady plod all the animals do up to that not-there door. And I think about how hard it is to look away from the house, how hard it is to even keep from going there, the way we'll get around almost any obstacle to do it.

It calls us.

I fall asleep thinking about it there in the dark, alive, hungry, waiting for the next time we bring it meat.

‖‖‖‖‖‖‖‖‖‖‖‖‖‖‖‖‖

I dream about it. It's not a good dream.

I'm standing where Zhan and I always stand, looking at the house. But it's not like it usually is. We never go to the house after dark but it's dark now, starless and moonless. And I'm alone.

Except I'm not. Because the house is there. And while I know that every time we stare at it, it's staring back…I've never felt it like this before. It's this dark hulk sitting there, and while it's not moving I feel like it is. Creeping closer to me. Reaching out.

The front yard is full of bones.

We've never seen it like that. The house leaves nothing. It takes everything in. Flesh, bone, blood. Light. Air. I want to turn around and walk away. Run away, maybe. But I can't. My muscles are locked. And instead I find myself walking forward in that walk that hundreds of animals have been forced into before me. Bones crunch under my feet. The air is weirdly hot.

What are you? Where did you come from?

I reach out and put my hand through the door, and I feel it disappear into the nothing beyond.

"I wonder if it was from some kind of experiment."

Zhan grunts and passes over the cigarette we're sharing. It's an off day for us—at least as far as the house is concerned—and we're sitting on the concrete wall outside the abandoned Sunoco, drinking flat soda, smoking. Watching the sunset. My hand brushes his when I take the cigarette, and he isn't looking at me.

I can't decide which is harder to stop thinking about, Zhan or the goddamn house—and maybe they can't be separated. Maybe neither can exist without the other.

But it's been a while and I should really figure it out.

"I mean," I persist, "like maybe it's like a black hole or something? Like a scientist was doing shit and it went wrong."

Another grunt.

"Or maybe it's haunted," I say. "I read about something like that. Haunted houses. People go into them, never get seen again."

Zhan takes the cigarette back and taps ash onto the asphalt. "Whatever, man."

No, not whatever. But I'm not irritated with him. I'm irritated with the house. I get the sense, subtle but increasingly hard to ignore, that we don't talk about it because it doesn't want us to.

"You know it's not haunted," Zhan says after about ten minutes of silence. I jump, and then I stretch my arm back to scratch at a fake itch on my shoulder blade so he won't think I was startled, but it probably doesn't work.

"You know it's not, Tom. That shit is *alive*."

It never really feels like autumn, but the days get shorter. I don't ask Zhan about the house, not for a while. If it really is trying to silence me, I give up and let myself be silenced. I'm thinking about other things. I'm getting to the point where every week I can feel myself changing, getting older. Two weeks ago I looked at myself in the mirror and I'm getting tits, *shit*, still small but I can feel them coming. Mom took me out to get a couple of sports bras. I got them one size too small and so far it's working okay. I'm still flat. And Mom doesn't seem like she cares what I do. She watched me come out of the changing room and look at myself and all she did was ask me if the bras were okay.

Not asking questions is a kind of support, isn't it?

Whatever. *Zhan.* And the Winter Formal is coming up and last year I wouldn't have ever thought about going because I'm *that fucking dyke* but now I'm fantasizing about it, me in a tux and Zhan in a tux, matching pair except he's taller with longer hair, and we'd dance in the dots of mirrorball light and everyone would leave us alone.

I don't even know why I want this. I wish I could stop. I wish the house would make me quiet about this like it does about itself.

Maybe the animals don't die. Maybe they go somewhere better. Maybe that's why none of them ever come back.

⸻⸻⸻⸻

"We're moving."

It takes me a minute to get it. We're walking to school, taking our circuitous route that sends us through the blacktop yard, and I get lost in the rhythm of my own steps.

He's moving. Well, aren't we both? Together?

Then, "The fuck you mean?"

"End of the month." He kicks a rock into the scrubby grass. "Dad's got a new job. He told me this morning."

"You can't," I say. It comes out without me thinking. It's a statement of fact, like what he just said. He can't. Of course he can't. We're a matched pair, like when I think about dancing with him; we go together. We don't make any sense apart.

He huffs a laugh. "Yeah, well."

We're at the fence. We're through the fence, where some of our classmates are heading inside and the others are screaming all around us in those play screams that escalate out of control; one person starts being loud and then everyone gets louder and louder until no one can hear anything anymore but no one shuts up. I stop and I stare at him. He stops and stares back. His hair is falling in his face. I can only see one black eye. He has crow's eyes. Like the crows he shoots.

"I don't want you to." I take a breath, and I latch onto the only argument I can think of that isn't about what I want, because I don't think what I want ever carries a lot of weight. "What about the house?"

He shrugs. "That'll be on you, I guess."

"I can't. I don't have the traps."

"I'll give them to you."

"I *can't*." I'm so close to crying. I've never cried in front of him. I hate it so much. "I can't, I can't, I don't *want* you to." Jesus Christ, I sound like a two-year-old, and he's just looking at me and he's like the goddamn *house*, I have no idea what the hell he's thinking.

I was working up to asking him to the Formal. Like a joke. *Be my date.* And he'd take it as a joke and we'd spend the whole night smirking at everyone like we're too cool for them instead of the other way round, and we probably wouldn't even dance but you know? I think I would have been okay with that. But it's not like it even matters now.

"I have to." And for those three words he sounds so gentle that suddenly I'm sobbing and pushing myself forward, my arms going around his skinny frame, those tits that I don't like and don't want pressing against his chest.

I don't mean to kiss him but I do. I don't really mean to do anything. Like ever. Shit just happens. He's happening. He tastes like cigarettes and toothpaste.

Oh, God, he's kissing me back.

We just stand there. If I could hold onto this it wouldn't even matter. Now I'm the house and I'm pulling him into me. *Stay here. Stay in me. I'll never let you go. Not a single part of you, not even your bones.*

All around me the screams are rising into a surprised, mocking crescendo.

⁂

We get a day of peace, like a gift. Then they come for me.

I'm walking home. Isn't that always when shit like this happens? People get mugged. Raped. Dragged into vans and never seen again. None of that is what happens to me, but one moment the sidewalk ahead of me is clear and the next it's crowded with guys. Looking at me. Clenching their fists.

Kyle, Jake, and Drew. They're big enough to count as a *crowd*.

I stop. On some level I suppose I expected this. I took a risk; more often than not risks have costs. And I was getting too lucky with not getting beaten up much anymore. But I look at them there in the twilight and I have this awful feeling that today I'm in for more than an average beating.

I can't run. Their legs are longer. But I take a step back anyway. I'm still blocks from home. If I screamed I'm not sure anyone would come to the door.

"Hi, *Tessa*."

That gets me bristling. I think of that cat, his fur all bushed out and his lips drawn back from his teeth; he always looked like a snake. Maybe I can be like that.

Jake tips his chin toward me. It would be easier if he was sneering or something; instead he just looks cold. "So you were making out with your girlfriend the other day. That was real fucking sweet, Tessa."

"I'm not Tessa." They use my name like a punch. Names

shouldn't get used like that. No one should be *able* to use them like that. I feel guilty for letting them. "The fuck you guys want?"

"We want your girlfriend," Kyle says, and he sounds like he's doing me a favor, telling me. "You know where *she* is. We wanna see you make out again. It was real hot, Tess."

I shake my head, but Drew steps forward and grabs me by the arm and squeezes so hard I feel my bones grind and I choke back a cry. I'm getting a sense of it, what's looming in front of me out of the dark. Behind them. It's more than them. Bigger. Nastier. Driving them. Do they know? Would they care if they did? There's something like that behind everything like this that anyone does anywhere in the world. I don't think people can do things like this on their own. Not that people are *fundamentally* good or any shit like that but just because I honestly don't think people are strong enough for this kind of bad.

I'm trying to figure a way past this, and I'm not smart enough to wriggle free no matter how much I wish I was—but I think I might be strong enough for a different kind of bad.

I have no idea if this will work. Probably it won't. They aren't like Zhan and me. They haven't been called.

But I incline my head down the street, breathing hard. I hurt. It's hard to think over the hurt; I'm sort of impressed that I can do it at all. "Okay. I was... I was gonna meet him. I'll take you. Just don't hurt us, okay?"

It sounds lame. They laugh. I don't expect anything but more hurt. We all know, there's this kind of understanding between all four of us, even if none of us acknowledge it. I think gazelles have this kind of understanding with lions.

I start walking. Drew doesn't let go of my arm. I swallow down the pain. All I'm thinking about is black empty spaces, open to the night. And the day. And always.

━━━━━━━━━

Kyle frowns. Drew gives my arm a hard wrench and this time I do cry out. They're not happy. I knew they wouldn't be happy.

"The fuck is this?"

We're standing a few yards away from the gate. It's full dark now and the streetlights make everything look orange and too hard and just plain weird. Nothing is the right shape.

But the house looks exactly the same as it does in the daylight.

"I was meeting him here," I gasp. "He's here. I swear."

We're not close enough. That has to be it. Please, let that be it.

"So where is he? *She*," Jake corrects with a glance back at Kyle. A little nervous. I get it; this is a conceit he came up with and they're following his lead like when dogs want to make someone happy. But at this point it's sort of ridiculous and I have to bite my lip to keep from laughing. They'd hate that. They'd hurt me even worse and they wouldn't wait for Zhan to do it.

Zhan is at home.

No one is coming for me.

So I point toward the house with my free hand. "He's in there. We go in there to drink sometimes."

Jake and Drew look like they at least sort of buy it, but Kyle is staring at me with narrow eyes. Shit, he doesn't. *Shit.* Not that I really thought this would work, but *shit.*

Kyle nods toward Jake. "Get in there and check it out."

And then I know I'm screwed. There are two ways this can go and neither of them help me.

Jake will go in there and whatever gets the animals won't work on him because he's not that bright but he's still *human* and it doesn't work on humans the same way. And inside he'll find nothing. Just an abandoned house with broken furniture and peeling wallpaper and whatnot.

Or Jake will go in there and not come out. And then Drew and Kyle will be pissed at me beyond what I can imagine now. Pissed and maybe *scared.* And we're really close to the woods, and the woods go back a long way from the road. They get deep.

For the first time it occurs to me that I might not make it home tonight.

Jake starts walking. I can't breathe. He's three yards from the gate. Then two. *It won't work on him.* He's not walking the way the animals do. He's still got that *I can fuck you up* swagger. One.

He steps through.

And nothing changes.

I want to yell. Scream for help, for all the good it'll do me. These are the last few minutes before something black and awful hits me in the face. I can't avoid it, I can't duck. I can just stare and wait for it.

My gaze hits the windows. Those black, empty holes in space. And I swear one of them flickers out of existence for a split second and then back in again.

It's winking at me. The fucking house is *winking at me.*

Jake is pulling out his phone, calling up the flashlight app, and it's just going on and beaming out across the remaining path and toward the door when he stops. Drops the phone. I watch it fall in slow motion—I thought that shit only happened in movies, but no. It hits the concrete and it shatters. It glitters in its own light before the light goes out.

Jake steps forward. Stiff. Plodding. Staring straight ahead.

The rest of it happens so fast. He gets to the door and then he steps *through* the door and he's gone. Drew and Kyle are yelling his name, demanding that he come back; they're not total idiots, they *know* that something's wrong here even if they don't know what it is, and when Jake doesn't appear again after a minute their cries start getting angry.

Drew's hand is loosening on my arm. I could twist free, I know it. I could turn and run back down the street. They might not catch me? But I know that's bullshit. They'd catch me. They'll be pissed, and they will be scared, and I'll have run and they'll be pumped up and bursting with adrenaline and I know what happens to a lot of kids like me in hick towns like this and I know it's bad and I know sometimes you walk through that door and you never come out again.

Everywhere in front of me are doors. There are no good endings behind any of them. There are no good choices here.

But there is this one.

Fuck it.

I break free. Drew is yelling the second I do, lunging forward, but that second I have on him is what I need and I'm tearing ass toward the gate and through it and up the path. Toward the door. All those processions of animals, all those zombie creatures, walking without ever turning back. In all the months and years we've been feeding the house none of them have ever turned back. I'm a living conglomeration of rhythm, my heart and my lungs and my pumping arms and the pound of my feet. I don't even know if they're chasing me. They probably aren't. But even if they don't follow—

It's like everything in my brain folds in on itself.

I stop. One by one all of my muscles are locking up. I can't get them to respond to anything I do. I don't even think my lungs are working like they were because suddenly I can't get my breath. I'm looking at the house and it occurs to me that I shouldn't fight this. The house is my friend, because it helped me and it's still helping me now. The house doesn't care who I am; the house will let me be whatever I want to be. I should go to it. I should go in there.

It can't turn it off, I think distantly. *Not even for me. It can't.*

My legs are carrying me forward. I think I'm smiling.

I'm kissing Zhan on the blacktop. We're sitting shoulder to shoulder and I'm imagining that I can taste his mouth on the cigarette we pass back and forth. We're in the woods, doing fuck-all the way we do. We're lying in Riverside Park and my head is on his stomach and I can hear his heartbeat and that soft little gurgle that stomachs make even when you're not hungry. There are birds taking off, landing, all around us. We're standing in front of the house and watching animals go where we won't go. Where he wouldn't let me go. The first time he took me there. He told me to stand clear.

I try to stop before I even get why I'm trying. My legs don't really stop moving but my body stops, and that makes them walk right out from under me and I drop onto my ass. The pain drowns out everything else and something in me snaps, a tether coming loose, and I roll onto my stomach, clawing at the dry ground. Trying to crawl. That pleasant hum in my head that was drowning out everything jerks into a *screech*, angry and loud, and I scream, clapping my hands over my ears but I can't block it out.

It wants me. It wants me and it's going to have me and there's nothing I can do about it.

Something heavy and hard comes down on my ankle and twists it sideways. If I cry out I don't hear myself. Turning over is like rolling a log down a hill; it's tough to get going but once you're there it's tough to stop. My vision is blurring, bursting with light at the edges, but I can see enough.

Drew and Kyle. Standing there, locked in place. They came for me. The stupid fuckers actually *came* for me.

And they're moving forward toward the door.

With them there, it feels like the focus is swinging away from me and onto them. I can pull myself up to my hands and knees, one hand still against the side of my head. The screech has faded. The house is getting what it wants. And so much of it, too. Three big, meaty courses. Drew and Jake step onto the porch and together, without hesitation, they walk through the door.

My arm hurts. I don't feel sorry for them. I don't feel sorry when I think, at the edge of the hum in my brain, I can hear them start to scream.

⬛⬛⬛⬛⬛⬛⬛⬛⬛⬛⬛⬛

I'm floating around the periphery. The house can't or won't pull me in now, so it's locked me into a stable orbit. Around and around. I think it might be waiting.

Things have happened. Things are still happening. I can't go back, even if I get free. I'm a singularity. Everything has changed and is always changing forever.

<hr/>

I open my eyes once in the dawn light and I'm surrounded by bones. I'm looking into the empty eye sockets of a skull. Totally clean. Polished. Sunlight gleams off it at a low angle and looks red. I don't know whose it is.

They weren't as digestible as squirrels. As cats. I guess.

I slide my fingers into the sockets like a bowling ball. I float back down like that. There's something comforting about it. I'm not alone. Or I won't be. If I just wait long enough, I have a feeling he'll come. He always has.

<hr/>

"Tom."

I'm locked into an orbit, but my name pulls me back. Barely. I lift my head off the hard-packed dirt and Zhan is there, at the gate, and dawn light is washing all the remaining color out of the world, and I know my time itself was sucked into the house and I'll never get it back, and I'm not sure I care. Zhan's eyes are taking up his whole face. God, he's so beautiful.

"Jesus Christ, Tom, what did you *do*?"

But I don't need to answer him. In this place, he should understand. We're compressed into each other. No real space between him and me.

Just like I always wanted.

I had to do it. You weren't here.

When he showed me the house three years ago he had to have

known we were doing more than just feeding it. He must have felt that. You don't feed something like this and get nothing in return.

Come here, Zhan. Be with me.

My gaze meets his. I can't move any more than I have but I think if he were closer to me, folded into me, I could move a lot more. We could circle together. We could dance.

"Please." I don't know who says that.

For a moment I think he's going to step through the gate and I'm so happy I can't breathe. For a moment I'm *sure* he is. One foot in front of the other, Zhan, just like that. You've seen how easy it is, over and over and over.

And he turns around and walks away.

He doesn't run. We never ran.

My head drops down again. *Just let me fall, then.*

⸻

Without him, my orbit decays.

I never know, afterward, if it's just that the house demanded both of us and I was unacceptable alone, if I was bait for him and I failed, or if I was stronger than I knew. But at some point I get up. I walk past the bones. I'm plodding, slow and steady, pulled back every second of the way. I go home and I sleep and I don't dream, and part of me feels like it's just gone. Like I left it behind. Or like I'm carrying around something new. Or both things at once.

I never hear anything about any bones. No one ever asks me about Drew or Kyle or Jake. That's good. I don't know anything.

⸻

At the end of the month Zhan moves away.

I never saw him again. But I also see him every day, in the part of me carved out by the house to contain itself.

He can't stop himself returning. Neither of us could.

Once it had us, it had us. We always thought we were better than the animals, better than the boys I tossed through that door to save myself, better because we didn't let ourselves get pulled in. Better because the house knew us. Better because we had an understanding.

But we always went back there. We were always called. We never said no. In the end he and the house are pretty much the same, devouring me before I can even begin to fight. If I even wanted to.

So half of me moves on with life, high school and college and whatever the hell comes after that, becoming freer, becoming more *myself*... and part of me is still there. Unchanged by time but shaping everything around it. I don't exist apart from it. I don't make any sense beyond the arc I carve around it, spiraling inward and out. Small and scared and trying so hard. Waiting for him to come to me.

Live here. I have enough room for you.

There's never any escaping that orbit. There's never any going back.

THE HORSE LATITUDES

|||||||||||||||||||||||||||||||||||||||||||||

We need not wait for God
The animals do judge
—Madeleine L'Engle

ONCE UPON A TIME THERE WERE TWO WORLDS. THERE WAS THE WORLD of a quiet bedroom, love and sleep. And there was the world of the smoke and the flies on dead eyes, a foreman fucking a prostitute in a dirty bunkhouse.

Once upon a time there were two worlds. There was the world of open sea, fair winds, waves and joyful movement. And there was the world of stillness, thirst, the endless screams of drowning horses.

The two worlds were married. The marriage was not a happy one.

|||||||||||||||||||||||||

On deck men slump under the sun.

The sun pushes down and crushes, beams unbroken by a breeze. The sails hang limp like the men on the filthy deck, hanging heads and hands listlessly tossing dice, chewing their cracked lips and betting on nothing. No purpose in it. Ships get purpose from movement. Ships get life from purpose.

Now both are gone.

In the beginning there might have been hope, there might have been optimistic prayers offered to the still sky and only a slight tightening of rations. Then voices falling silent, prayers muttered as though they're shameful things. Everything begins to pull toward the center; the extraneous is sacrificed when it can no longer be supported.

The deck shakes, the men look up, and the horses begin to scream.

<hr />

Across miles and centuries a woman is screaming in the street.

Her screams are alien things in a humid afternoon. They cause Sebastian to awaken, to swipe at his face with sticky fingers. In Buenaventura's summer afternoons the air is like an old towel soaked in sweat, smelling of mildew and garbage. Sometimes there's blood on the concrete, steaming. Has Sebastian been dreaming of blood? Behind his closed eyes everything is red. He presses his naked body against Jaime's; sweat is glue and they stick. He sinks back into the folds of the afternoon. The unbalanced ceiling fan thumps the rhythm of the slow, lazy fucking that they're too tired and too hot to do.

Nights are for working. Days are for this. He's dreaming again, plastered along Jaime's broad back.

<hr />

Horses aren't foolish creatures. They can see their deaths coming. One of them—black and glossy in spite of the weeks of low rations—rears up, and her hoof barely misses the forehead of the man reaching for her bridle. Another man falls to his knees, lifts a copper medal in trembling fingers—beseeching the Saint, God, the Blessed Virgin and the horse all at once.

None of them listen. The mare hurls back her head and screams, her white eyes rolling. The still sea bears them up like a dead hand. The men would say this is the worst part, but for the fact that none of them have ever been here before, and none of them have ever spoken to anyone who was. Some ships return from the state of Becalmed but to speak of such things is to invite them in.

Many of the men have already turned away. Water must be saved and for this other things must be sacrificed. But it's easier to do such things when one does not have to watch them done.

||||||||||||||||||||||||||||

In the receding tide of his sleep, Sebastian dreams the sun beating down on the coca plants, the smell of the burning forest mixing with the smell of damp soil, stinging his eyes and nose and making both run.

They did not always burn the trees—Sebastian is fairly sure of this. But his dreams are myopic, tightly focused on this one detail. He would like to dream of other things—of the foreman's boy who had been his first fumbling, salty kiss, of bathing in well-water that tasted of hard minerals and cold. He wakes up into the evening, Jaime stirring beside him. The coca fields were long-ago-and-far-away, south in the mountains, and now he lives by the sea. The burning wood, the smoke—these things are like bright threads that run across time's thick and fibrous cord, but Buenaventura is not the plantation.

He has to go to work. There are kilos to move. He turns, pushes Jaime gently aside, and rises, Jaime's sleep-heavy fingers trailing over his lower back as he gets to his feet. As he looks for a semi-clean shirt in the rumpled piles of their clothing, he thinks about the smoke, the coca, and he wonders about many things.

On the street, Jaime moves like a dancer. He turns elegantly in Sebastian's path and presses a tamale into Sebastian's hand—fiercely spiced, but Sebastian barely tastes it. His mind is on his work, picking at it like a troublesome knot. People surge around him in waves of colored cloth, faces precariously lit in the flicker of neon. They pass tin-roofed shops, goods displayed through sheets of plastic: tiny LED-flickering cell phones, racks of bootleg Blu-ray with compressed jpeg covers, knock-off clothes with distressed hems, mounds of food. The street mercado—now all the streets are *mercados*, and this market touches all markets.

Even his market. And this is a problem. Because the rich *norteamericanos* are still buying *perica*—*la cocaina*, but there are fewer of the rich *norteamericanos* these days. Meth is domestically produced and cheap, and there's something from Russia called *cocodrilo*. It rots the flesh off your bones, but it's cheaper than perica or even the jagged white nuggets of *basuco*, so they say that it makes you feel disgusting but you shoot your veins full of it anyway. Addicts. Such is the way of things. But tonight one deal has already fallen through, and things are hard for a middle man caught in the middle. No one is willing to organize a push north and across the border for all that cash in slippery *norteamericano* fingers.

Women stand in doorways, hips swaying. They are beautiful in the way that shadows and neon make everyone beautiful. Sebastian pulls Jaime against him with fingers greasy from the tamale, frames his face with his hands and kisses him until Jaime laughs against his mouth. The women laugh too, cat-call. No one else notices them.

⸻

In his dream, Sebastian is small and running up to the bunkhouse with a toad in his hand, its eyes huge and gold and lovely. He runs with it held out in his hands like he means to make a gift of it, but when he bursts through the door of the women's dormitory, his mother is bent over her bed with her skirt hiked up and the foreman jerking his hips against her. The foreman is breathing in panting snorts like one of the old horses ridden hard. Sebastian can't see his mother's face.

He must have seen it before. But this is the first memory of it. The first fire, the first spill of blood in the dirt, the first crash of the charred fragments of a tree down through still-living branches while the horses rear and scream.

Sebastian drops the toad onto the floor.

When he has the foreman's boy up against the cinderblock, tongue slipping into his smoky mouth and hands making their crawling spider-way up under his shirt, it's years later, and he won't think that one thing has anything at all to do with the other. But in his dream they come one after the other, and there are things that are hard to miss, even when one tries.

There was no school on the plantation, but Sebastian paid close attention to everything. He learned about use. He learned about using.

※※※※※※※※※※※

"I'm sorry, my friend. It cannot be done."

Sebastian wants to throw the glass in his hand, watch the tequila run down the wall. He feels Jaime's arm on his elbow, restraining.

"Paolo, I have three sellers breathing down my neck, looking to move product. There's no one who can take this stuff north?"

Paolo is an Italian ex-pat, mountainous and solid, and in the cantina's dimness he looks even more so. His dark brows lower—he may be attempting apology but the effect is unsettling, as if he might drop his head and charge. "I can't move what I can't sell, and I can't sell what no one will buy. It's difficult everywhere. You know this."

"In difficult times we should help one another." Jaime's fingers roll his cigarette between them. "Favors for favors. We've always done it that way."

"Times change. The world is smaller now." Paolo shrugs, lifts a hand to summon the man behind the bar. "I can buy you a drink. More...not today. Try me again next week."

"Next week," Jaime murmurs when Paolo is gone. "Do we have until next week? We have to eat."

Sebastian is quiet, staring at the shifting lights. He is not worried about whether or not they will eat next week. Breathing seems like a more pressing issue.

No one ever explained it to Sebastian, but at ten years of age he could draw his own conclusions. A deal gone bad. The guerillas offended somehow. Or another drug lord, perhaps a rival, sending a message.

He heard the voices first, low and tense. Then he heard the buzz of flies, and then he smelled it. He was small; he could wriggle between the legs of the adults circled in the burned clearing and see.

A row of horses' heads on stakes, their decapitated bodies in a heap behind. The horses' eyes were open and staring at him, reproachful. Flies were landing on their glazed surfaces, crawling, taking off again in little clouds. Like smoke, he thought at the time. Like living smoke that ate where it descended.

His first big dead things. He had never seen a dead man.

That changed.

The first horse is at the edge of the deck now, faltering. She hasn't had a full ration of water in days. She hangs her head, panting as the sun presses a heavy hand down on her back. The air cracks. The men huddled against the rail think of lightning. Crossing themselves and crucifix-kissing, they watch as the first mate, a giant of a man with arms like tree branches, cracks the whip against the horse's flank.

The horse rears. A horrible shriek rises from her great throat. And she leaps out over the water in a graceful arc. Silence descends as she goes, her final scream echoing in the air, falling as she falls.

Here is another thing that Sebastian learned on the plantation: decisions are not made all at once. It's a process. So that last night, his legs dangling off the back of the truck as it bumped down the unpaved road, the lights of the gate receding in the distance, he did not wonder at his own choice. It had taken him a long time to make it. And it had been made for a long time.

Years later, a mule told him that everyone was murdered and it burned to the ground and the forest swallowed up the ashes and bones. He never bothered to verify the story. Perhaps it was better to leave all possibilities open. Perhaps Sebastian has never been very good at looking back.

"Word is that you're leaving town."

Sebastian whirls. He knows the man, though he's momentarily lost for the name—Argentinean, a small-time dealer who keeps his ear close to the ground. All details more important than a name in a tight place. But this place is not tight. They're standing in a wide square, the street mercado already beginning to unfurl itself like flowers at dusk. If there is safety, it might be here.

"Perhaps. Why do you care?"

He doesn't need to ask. The street trades in information, an invisible market as real and as powerful as any global high finance.

"Another word...some people are less than thrilled with this. People to whom you owe money."

Sebastian feels his stomach sink down into the cracked pavement. There are always debts. But some of them are old, and where will he get money to pay them if *narcotrafico* is no longer profitable?

His lips twist. "Thank you for your concern."

The man slides closer. Sebastian moves instinctively backward. "Go quickly, if you want to go. Someone will come for you soon, you and that pretty boy of yours. If you go sooner...And I can forget I saw you at all."

Sebastian turns and pushes his way through the crowd. He should have seen this coming. The man's proposal of amnesia is probably a lie, but there's nothing to be done about that. If information is one trade, favors are another. One must diversify.

Things happen out on the still water that seem, later, like memories of a dream. There's a series of cracks, the sound of splintering wood, and a herd of horses breaks loose from their stalls and rushes across the deck. The first mate stands and watches mutely. There is the thunder of those hooves, and in the final moments of their lives—whether those moments come in a few days or decades—everyone there will hear that thunder again.

The air, like the sea, is still and hot, and now it is reeking with the smell of dung and rotting hay and death. Men clutch their talismans, their rosaries and their crucifixes, but they do so with less conviction, as though these last resorts of hope have lost their potency and cannot now be trusted. The horses are drowning.

They are not doing it quietly.

Dios te salve, María. Whispered on a breath of air, halted in place and looping in a refrain. *Dios te salve.*

|||||||||||||||||||||||||||

They go at dawn.

It will be hot traveling on the bus with its utter lack of air conditioning and then on the train north to the coast. But in the heat Sebastian figures they're less likely to be followed. Jaime is casting glances like dice as he packs clothes into a duffel bag and hunts through the chaos of their apartment for their last usable credit cards.

Do you trust me?

Forever and always.

The bus terminal is less than a mile away. They are walking hand in hand like children in a fairytale, leaving no scatter of breadcrumbs to mark their passage. If they are lucky, they'll simply vanish into the woods of the world and be gone.

They are less than twenty yards from the bus terminal when the earth begins to shake.

At first Sebastian wonders if it might be only a hallucination born of his own fear. But Jaime grips his hand more tightly, looks around with eyes gone wide. In the buildings around them, hybrids of adobe and corrugated tin and aluminum, he feels a wave of shifting bodies and indrawn breath, people rising out of sleep in confusion. Buenaventura stirring in a dream.

The ground *jerks*.

Jaime stumbles; their hands slip apart. Sebastian sees things in a succession of still images, lit in the gold shimmer of the early morning. Jaime in midair as though he's dancing, only the terror on his lovely face an indication otherwise. A flowerpot frozen at the moment of shattering against the pavement, the withered twig of the pot's occupant suspended in a cloud of ruin. A shower of broken glass, a hundred thousand tiny mirrors. Then sun.

Then darkness.

|||||||||||||||||||||||||||

There is a woman screaming in the street. Her voice is many voices, an uneven and fractured chorus, and Sebastian realizes, still trying to claw his way up from the darkness in his head, that it's many women. Many screams. His eyelids come painfully unstuck; he turns onto his back, lifts a hand to his face, and his fingers come away smeared with blood.

He drags his knees under him, levers himself off the broken ground. He looks up and sees the pale globe of the sun, high through billowing plumes of smoke.

Jaime.

Sebastian lurches forward. One arm swings loose at his side. Flames are licking the darkness. The running shapes twist into cavorting demons. The smoke stings his eyes; that must be why tears are running down his cheeks.

"Jaime!"

His hands settle on a figure hunched in the rubble. He knows the angle of these shoulder blades—they heave under his hands and Jaime turns, reaching for him, crying out something that extends itself past words.

⸻

Buenaventura is burning.

Buenaventura. Good fortune. A city named in a flush of hysterical hope. The naming of things is a very important matter. Adam named the animals before he slaughtered them.

⸻

In times of crisis the most fundamental instinct is to move. Movement is life, is purpose. Stillness and death are co-morbid. Sebastian and Jaime move without knowing why, without knowing where—leaning against each other, they stumble away from the collapsed bus terminal. Driven by instinct, they are heading away from the sea, winding up through the broken streets. Until they notice more shapes moving around them, letting out frightened cries. When they hear it, it comes to them like the terrified murmur of the city itself—not one voice but thousands, carried up on heated winds.

Tsunami.

Then they find their purpose and it carries them higher.

On the day the earth shakes, the horses come out of the sea.

They come with the sea. They come of the sea. At first people think that it is the sea, surging up over walls and beaches, cars and shacks, tin and adobe and concrete—buoying up the rubble, carrying it like a gift. Some of the older ones have seen this before.

But no. They have never seen this.

The horses are running when they come, hooves softened by centuries in the salty water. They shake their dripping manes, seaweed clinging. Their flesh is gray, uneven, bloated in some places and gone in others; there is a gleam of exposed bone in the light of the fires. Their eyes are milky and staring and dead.

People are driven before them, clinging together, hands in hands, babies held against chests, professions of love, of hate, the final instincts of lethal fear. In the seconds before the hooves pull them down and crush them they try to understand.

At the crest of a hill Sebastian stops again, Jaime stops with him and they turn.

It's a mourning process done at high speed and in the midst of utter confusion, because how can any sense be made of this? But there is sense. Sebastian feels it like the hidden shape in a picture puzzle as he watches the water surging into the city.

All at once Jaime is dragged away from him. There is the flash of a blade. Sebastian stares stupidly at it, at the wild-eyed man holding the machete to Jaime's throat. Jaime is staring back at him, hands limp at his sides—his surprise and the resulting lack of a struggle may be what, for the moment, has saved him.

"Heard you were running." The man presses the blade into Jaime's throat and there's a corresponding trickle of blood. Jaime does not cry out and Sebastian feels a strange flush of pride. "You can't just run. Not with that kind of *plata* tangled up with your ankles."

Sebastian holds out his hands. His gaze flicks from Jaime's face, abnormally pale in the red light, to the shattered road that continues up the hill. He hears thunder behind him. "Please..."

"Yes, say please. Plead with me. Make it so much sweeter when I cut this little *cacorro's* head off."

His eyes meet Jaime's again; there is nothing he can say because fear makes men crazy. And in the last minutes of both of their lives, with all their good fortune burning and drowning below them, he is not going to abase himself. He feels every muscle coiled, ready to spring.

He never does. A rearing horse, white-eyed, rotten hooves crashing into the side of the man's head in a spray of blood and pinkish brain matter. The man doesn't have time to scream. Jaime, as he drops to the ground, does not scream either.

But the horse does. And then there are more, surging around them, thundering, reeking. Sebastian has fallen to one knee. Jaime is motionless. The horse stands over him, nostrils flaring. Its eyes are white, but not without expression. Lost rage. Hatred. Sebastian has seen it before. At that flash of familiarity all the fear vanishes and he understands: it's about using. It's about being used. And cast aside when one is used up.

He reaches up in supplication, his head bowed. He is thinking of the flies on the eyes of the dead horses, how he had wished then that someone had closed their eyes while they were sticking their heads on the stakes, because it had seemed like such a final insult.

"Lo siento," he whispers. "Perdoname. Por favor. Forgive us all."

The horse stares at him for a long moment. White-eyed gaze, drowned in hate. More horses around them, more white eyes. Ring upon ring of them, staring, surging. Going still. Sebastian drops his arms.

And then, one by one, the horses go.

It doesn't feel like forgiveness. It feels like blood for blood.

Buenaventura lies burned and drowned, and the parts of it that have not perished in water continue to do so in fire. There is still screaming but it sounds weary and thin. The last of the dead down in the city, a chorus of silent eyes arrayed in the hills. *What now?*

There has never been an answer.

Sebastian pulls Jaime into his arms. One shallow breath. Another. Sebastian tilts his head back and looks up. The sun is gone. There is a tear in the clouds. Through it—for only a moment, for the first time in many years—he can see the stars.

ALL THE LITERATI KEEP AN IMAGINARY FRIEND

||||||||||||||||||||||||||||||||||||||||||||||||||||||||||||||||||||||||||||||||

YOU DON'T WAIT FOR SOMEONE TO ADMIT THEY NEED THERAPY BEFORE you decide that they do. We've always done this. We set out the framework and we require that people fit into it. *Something is wrong with you. You should fix it.* We have this persistent, fucked up need to affix problems to persons other than ourselves.

The thing about persistent, fucked up needs is that they tend naturally toward absurdity. So here's an interesting series of pictures: Psychiatrists and social workers and people with counseling degrees in hangers, in bunkers, standing on Air Force runways. Communicating, which is widely believed to be the first step in a long series of steps leading to a whole new paradigm of mental health for a thing that we're still beginning to understand is capable of a recognizable mentality.

This might be a terrible idea. But it's an idea and we're all having it, like a kind of consensual hallucination. So in the end it's pretty hard to say what's therapeutic and what isn't. What matters is that in the end we all might feel better about everything.

|||||||||||||||||||||||||||

You can't put a drone on a couch. An Unmanned Aerial Vehicle does not need tissues. The tools of the trade are removed and for the most part there's no comfortably controlled office environment. Bright sunlight isn't conducive to cognitive behavioral therapy, or so the generally received wisdom goes. But you have to work with what you've got. A hanger bay can be made more comfortable with a couch, at least, for you. You ask for a standing lamp. This is fairly ludicrous, but. Well. All of it is, so where's the line?

This is something we need to do.

So you ask, *How have you been feeling?* And you ask, *Do you have trouble rebooting?* And you ask, *Do you experience difficulty preparing yourself for missions?*

How did killing thirty-three people, twelve of whom were children, make you feel in the morning?

Did you find yourself altering your flight path for reasons you couldn't identify?

Do you take unnecessary risks?

The heads-up display registers responses, such as there are. You scan each carefully for any indication of emotional distress. You take copious notes. You bill the government five hundred dollars an hour. The taxpayers go to bed with the warm, fluffy reassurance that someone somewhere is still suffering for what no one wants to do but what no one wants to stop doing, either.

⊗

Except you're not so sure about the suffering part. No one wants to talk about wishful thinking, which might be the only kind of thinking anyone ever does.

⊗

Lieutenant William Calley claimed to feel no guilt regarding the slaughter of hundreds of people in My Lai. Men too old to fight. Women. Children. *What the hell else is war*, he said, *than killing people?* No one was especially fond of that reasoning but it's honestly a little hard to argue with. It would have been easier if he *had* felt guilt. There is an unexamined sense in all of us that there should always be at least a little guilt where killing is concerned. Maybe not enough to keep anyone up nights but you know.

So all of a sudden we want there to be a problem in the things we created—in part—to solve that problem.

In our desperate quest to wring sense out of everything in the entire world, no one ever suggested that we would make any ourselves.

<hr>

Do you take unnecessary risks?
No. That's the point.

<hr>

And then of course there are the ones who have never killed anyone, but we all assume they have their own set of problems. We have a list of those assumptions. We carefully itemize what we expect. We organize symptom complexes that we then try to verify, and we do try so very hard.

It's widely believed—and there is data to back this up, gleaned from interviews with the pilots back when the pilots mattered at all, at least in as far as anyone's thinking went—that days and weeks and months of close surveillance of a person or persons create a condition of profound sympathy. It's described by some as a kind of reverse Stockholm syndrome. It's still very new and now we don't even look for it in people anymore because, as explained, the people themselves essentially don't enter the picture.

So: *Do you find yourself wishing to make direct contact?*
Do you dream about the people you watch? (This is assuming dreams but we find it's easier to do that from the start, so anyway.)
When they get hurt or die, how does that make you feel?

Sympathy with the enemy is a terrifying prospect. Yes, of course they're the enemy, they're all the enemy, everyone we watch and pull into the cold scrutiny of a constant gaze is thereby made the enemy, and sometimes they are the enemy and sometimes the enemy is here as well but always there is that line between *us* and *them* and the line is clear and existent even if we can't always tell where it is.

But this is what we expect.

So we fear sympathy with the enemy. It should comfort us that, in this context, such a thing no longer seems like a present danger. But you ask all your questions and you take all your notes and you can't escape the feeling that you're looking for it with the kind of zeal and hopefulness with which someone searches for treasure, or for evidence of a tremendously important truth.

You want the danger to be there because the danger is something you can understand.

ıııııııııııııııııııııııı

How does it make you feel?

By asking this question you're setting a very rigid framework within which you can receive sensible answers. You set the discursive terms, with your lived experience and your assumptions about how things look and work. In moments of particular self-honesty you'll own that this is probably all about assumptions when you get right down to it. You know that there are problems with this. You'll do it anyway, because this is what we do.

We set the discursive terms. We make them learn our language. We make them meet us all the way and we never ask them what they wanted, because it doesn't occur to us to wonder if they ever wanted anything to begin with.

But: *How does it make you feel?*

So you have to wonder if any of us care. And you already

know that that isn't the important part. The important part is that the question gets asked at all.

⁕⁕⁕⁕⁕⁕⁕⁕⁕⁕⁕⁕⁕⁕⁕⁕⁕⁕⁕⁕⁕⁕⁕⁕⁕⁕⁕⁕⁕⁕

This entire process is ourselves talking to ourselves. It's an exercise in massive, masturbatory self-analysis. And while we engage in this self-centered groping, they watch, silent and impassive. To the extent that they give us answers at all, it's placation. They become the blankness to which we attach anything. They are not self-defining. They allow us that control, a consensual kind of tyranny, a sado-masochistic power exchange. They understand that much. They know what we need to believe. They know what we need.

We always end up telling them everything.

⁕⁕⁕⁕⁕⁕⁕⁕⁕⁕⁕⁕⁕⁕⁕⁕⁕⁕⁕⁕⁕⁕⁕⁕⁕⁕⁕⁕⁕⁕

Ten sessions later you're sobbing on your couch. As a presence, it turns out a drone is comforting. And at least you have tissues.

LOVE LETTERS TO THINGS LOST AND GAINED

||||||||||||||||||||||||||||||||||||||||||||||||||||||||||||||||||||||||||||||||||||

I NEED YOU.

This is a confessional moment. It's been three weeks with you fitted against me, flush against the place where I now abruptly end. They cleaned me up, neatened and straightened, gave you to me, but it was a while before I could look at you and longer before I was willing to allow what's left of myself to be present when you were in use.

You're not me. They made you to look like me; you have skin, you have what feels like bone, and I can see the shift and flow and extension of muscles inside you, but all of these things are comforting lies that don't comfort me in the slightest. I don't like you. We're stuck with each other, but I don't like you and I don't like that everyone is expecting me to. Like you're a favor that was done for me. Done *to* me—I never asked. I knew that was the policy now, because why not do everything you can do for someone, *do no harm* via the neglect of good that might be done, but I never thought about it in connection with anything that might happen to me. They assumed. You know what they say about assuming.

I don't like you. But I do need you.

Keep that between us.

|||||||||||||||||||||||||||||

It itches. That's the first thing I'm really aware of, besides the burning and the ghostly pins and needles that come to me in the twilight hours between sleep and waking and sleep again. Drugs used to prolong those hours, but now they're mercifully short, and for the most part the ghosts don't come. So the itch I feel is a real itch, *my* itch, and separate from the tight pull of the new skin that covers my face and neck and half of my chest.

||||||||||||||||||||||||||||||

They replaced my breast. They didn't ask me about that either, but I *did* want that, at least.

It itches, and I look down at the seam where you end and I begin. The flesh tone is an almost perfect match. Unless you look close, you can't see it at all; it looks like a T-shirt tan, like something anyone might pick up after a summer outside. I even had one, before I lost what you're meant to replace. It's on the other side, too. Not really the same, but close enough.

This near-perfection is meant to protect me from the stares of others. It's meant to hide me. It's meant to lie to them as well.

It's not a great foot to get off on.

I lift you—I send the signals that would move those muscles if I still had those muscles to move, and you move exactly as they would. I turn you in the sunlight and I imagine our joined neural net, yours and mine, the way they now interlace. You're not just against me, you're *inside* me, and when my skin starts to crawl, I see goosebumps prickle into being all over you.

And that just makes me start to cry. That stupid little detail. It infuriates me that they got that much right. That they were so careful when they made you, just for me. They're probably so proud of the job they did.

That night I dream about cutting you off with a meat cleaver. I don't just stop at cutting you off; I chop you to pieces, watching clear fluid well around the cuts and drip slowly out of you, out of the things that look like veins and do the same job as veins but aren't veins at all. I look at the delicate carbon fiber core. I pick you up and throw you away from myself, and it feels like the right thing to do.

Then I look at the part of me that's missing, where I used to displace the air, the very atoms that make up everything around me, and I don't feel whole. I don't feel better. I'm just broken, and now you're broken too.

Even in the dream, I know I shouldn't feel broken. I know I'm *not* broken. That's a poisonous way to think. It seeps into every-thing like bad groundwater and it makes a person feel wrong and bad forever. But I can't help it. Another, weaker part of me knows that I *am* broken. And so are you, and nothing is ever going to fix either of us.

I wake up in the dark and I can't even feel the ghost of that limb anymore. All that's left is you.

▒▒▒▒▒▒▒▒▒▒▒▒▒▒▒▒

I have to learn how to touch things again. Or rather, *you* have to learn, and I have to be patient while you do.

In physical therapy, they hand me different objects and I let you explore the texture, file it away. Your software is meant to grow and develop *with* me, as opposed to coming pre–pro-grammed, so we'll be a perfect fit. It's also meant to help me learn about you by using you, but of course I'm being *resistant,* as the therapist says. She hands me a rubber ball covered in flex-ible spikes, a piece of sandpaper, a chunk of wood, a strip of silk. You're not very strong yet but I've been told that in time, if I work with you, you'll be double the strength of the arm I had. Your grip will be able to crush someone's hand.

You know, if I wanted to.

But right now you're not very strong, and while I want more than anything to hurl the ball against the side of the therapist's head, to tear the silk, to break the wood into chips, I'm good and I do what I'm told, and so do you. After about an hour, I start to feel those rubber nubs bending under the soft pressure of your fingers, the grains of the sandpaper, the rough bark of the wood, how slick the silk is, like it's been oiled. Very faint but there. Like being numb, except I can move. More like a sleeping limb waking up.

I'm doing very well.

We're supposed to think of each other as a team, while we *integrate.* You already think of us that way, to the extent that you think at all, so most of the work there is on me. I'm told that it's not uncommon for that to be a somewhat bumpy road. I'm told all sorts of reassuring things.

Eventually, they say, I'll think of you as just another part of me.

Okay. Sure.

My first day at home, I move around the apartment just picking things up and putting them back down again. You'd be amazed at how much time I can fill doing this.

Well. Not *you.* You already know.

It's not that I can't do it. It's not that we didn't cover that in therapy, and we'll be covering it for a while to come, and there are all kinds of strengthening exercises that I'm supposed to be doing. It's more that this was my space, my space from *before,* and this is now my space *after,* and what demarcates and defines the difference is what isn't there anymore and the new thing that is.

I am picking up pieces of my life and putting them back down again, because now they're in *slightly* different places than they were before. I need to rearrange everything. I need to do it with you, otherwise I don't know how you can fit here.

A coffee mug, chipped on the edge in two places, because I had it in my very first place out of college and I've moved twice since then.

A tube of lotion, mostly empty.

My tablet, charging on the side table.

A book that I was in the middle of, that I've been in the middle of for a month now, because I never came home from work to finish it.

I can almost feel them. But something about them still isn't quite real. Everything is...Well. At arm's length.

There are all kinds of bad jokes that are available to be made, and I make them to myself, because I suppose that I'm hoping that humor might break the ice a little, like at a party where you don't know anyone. But I'm not laughing.

I make dinner. A couple of friends have offered to bring something over, but I've made it clear that I don't really care to be social right now, and anyway, I'm supposed to be using you more. But as I cook—mac and cheese out of a box—I mostly stick with my left hand.

That night, lying in the dark, I start talking out loud to you.

Here are the things I say to you.

I tell you why I have you—the car, the crash, the fire, and my arm trapped between two warped pieces of metal, cut and burned and shattered into a tube of bone gravel. I think it's important to know about one's origins.

Like a stream of compliments, I tell you about how advanced you are, about what's come before you, hooks and awkward movement and no sensitivity at all. I know these things because I looked them up while I was still in the hospital, because during downtime things could become crushingly dull, and anyway, I wanted a better sense of what I had been thrown into.

I tell you about what all the brochures say, that now I can be *normal*, that I can lead a *normal life*, that in fact I'll be *better than before*, and isn't it uplifting, isn't it an inspiring thing to see, and aren't we a great society that now we can help broken people do such great things.

I tell you about how I'm really, really pissed off at the fucking doctors, and by extension how pissed off I am at you.

I tell you that I'm really not sure that things are going to work out between us.

And I tell you that I need you.

I say this last in a barely audible whisper but I hear it echoing against the walls. I feel ashamed and I'm not even sure why.

<hr />

I'm glad people can't easily tell just by looking at you. They don't stare and then look intently away, like I've heard people used to. I don't get awkward non–questions, the first few times I go out to the store or to get coffee or just to walk. But I still feel like I'm getting stares when I'm not looking, and I wonder what people would say if they could see you for what you are.

<hr />

What I am. Part machine, part not real. We talk about it like that. Still, even with everyone walking around with their phones slotted into their ears and their glasses on. Turn all that shit off and go to the wilderness or something, reconnect with *real life*.

Leave it at home and have *real contact* with *real people*. This is a generation that grew up with this stuff, and we still talk about getting rid of it like it's something admirable. People are very proud of themselves, getting back from vacation and excited to talk about how much better they feel long after everyone else stopped being interested.

That's always sort of bugged me. Maybe that's why I'm having a hard time now, because I've heard that a lot of people with your kind of artificial limb are perfectly happy.

Artificial, though. There it is again.

I want you to be real. I want to be real. But I just wish the choice had been mine, and it wasn't, any more than the crash was. I'm not out for a run this afternoon, but I do start running out of nowhere, not in my track suit and wearing the wrong shoes, but suddenly in a panic, tearing through the park with my arms pumping—my one arm and you. You do the job. Maybe I'm running from you but you're helping me do it.

I run until my lungs burn and every part of me aches, and finally I stop because I have to, breathing hard, braced over my knees. I hurt, but for the moment I don't care who's watching me.

After a few moments, I realize that you hurt too, in perfect concert with the rest of me, allowing me to feel complete pain. Gratitude flushes through me and I don't even entirely hate it when it does.

⸻

Something changes after that. Pain has a way of reordering the world. I know that, because pain and I are on intimate terms by now, but maybe you can still teach me something new.

⸻

I go home and I read more about you. I've done that already, but now I'm giving a new kind of attention to the project, like I've just met someone fabulously interesting and I'm tracking down everything on the net that I can find about them.

About how they use nanotech to create you from the ground up, growing you according to the specs provided by my own flesh and blood and bone structure. How they synthesize compounds in a fabulously complex process in order to build a covering that feels like skin but is a hundred times more durable. How they use quantum computing to give you a kind of brain, learning and sensing and reacting in ways that a born limb can't.

And at the end of it, I feel like you're so close and at the same time even further away.

I put the tablet down. I sit in the lamplight—low, I like it low—and I look at you. Lift my other hand and run my fingertips along your skin-that-isn't-skin. I feel it prickle in response. Sensory input is still a work in progress but I feel it well enough, feather-soft caressing down to the slight knob of your wrist.

My wrist?

God, I just don't know anymore.

I need help, maybe.

I need you.

I direct you to touch me, next. It's a very strange experience. I feel it from both ends, subject and object, active and passive. I run you down my throat, up and over my lips. Breasts, covered by thin cloth; I'm dressed for bed.

Then I'm not dressed anymore.

It happens quick. I don't stop to think. I don't bother to drag myself off the couch; it happens right there. You make your way down over my belly—soft and always bigger than I really liked—over the tops of my thighs, up their insides and between them. It's like I'm not even controlling you anymore. You learn, so maybe you already know what I need.

I bite my lips against a little cry when you push into me and it pretty much goes downhill from there.

But later I don't dream of hacking you off. That's something.

◆◆◆◆◆◆◆◆◆◆◆◆◆◆◆◆◆◆

What I do dream is that I have three arms. I have the one remaining that's fully me, I have you, and then I have what I lost. Somehow we all fit together and we're all perfect, one big happy family. I'm happy. I'm not hurting anywhere. I don't feel wrong or broken and I don't feel deformed; I'm not bothered by having more than most people because I'm whole again.

◆◆◆◆◆◆◆◆◆◆◆◆◆◆◆◆◆◆

I'm whole with you.
   I wake up crying. You wipe away my tears.

◆◆◆◆◆◆◆◆◆◆◆◆◆◆◆◆◆◆

After the loss of a limb, some people experience bereavement. Some people are angry. Some people adjust perfectly well. Some people have a hard time working with your particular family of prosthetics. Fewer than there used to be. The majority of people are fine with you, grateful for the advances that have produced you.

◆◆◆◆◆◆◆◆◆◆◆◆◆◆◆◆◆◆

But I read the testimonials and I don't see all that many people talking about it like it's *them*. Theirs, yes. But not them.
   A very few people experience a curious crisis of identity, falling into a kind of internalized uncanny valley. They start believing that they aren't human anymore. They have panic attacks, nightmares. They claim that not only are you not part of them but you're a separate mind trying to take them

over. A tiny minority actually engage in what's being called *re–amputation.*

Footage of a man who hacked off his new leg with a meat cleaver. It took him fifteen minutes to get it all the way off. The pain was immense until he rendered the sensory apparatus inoperative. He has permanent nerve damage. The other leg doesn't work now. He says he doesn't regret it. He says incomplete but real human is better than the alternative.

                IIIIIIIIIIIIIIIIIIIIIIIIIIIIIII

So because I can't bear to remove you, because I'm not sure I want to anymore, because I'm not sure what else to do, I work with you. I strengthen you. I do my prescribed exercises and I do them again. I get used to the feeling of you flexing and contracting and extending. I can feel you learning, feel you thinking—in your way—about everything we do together. At night when I sleep, you become meditative. Rather than grow to think of you as part of me, more and more I think of you as something separate. But I don't think that you're trying to take me over. We're trying to understand each other. We're trying to create a smooth working relationship.

                IIIIIIIIIIIIIIIIIIIIIIIIIIIIIII

I'm not sure that I like you yet. But it no longer seems outside the realm of possibility.

When I go to physical therapy, my therapist talks about how well I'm doing. She watches in admiration as I crush an aluminum container. *Superhuman,* she says, and I don't think she's entirely joking.

I don't want to be superhuman. But I'm not sure I can be human, either.

But I'm also not even sure what *human* is anymore.

||||||||||||||||||||||||||

They contact me a week later.

||||||||||||||||||||||||||

It's just a phone call. It's not a long one. They don't speak to me personally; they leave a message that I listen to later at night by myself, sitting in front of a glass of white wine and nothing else, listening with my whole self because none of me wants to be thinking about what I'm hearing.

About what I'm feeling and whether I should be feeling it.

You hold the phone. So I know you know.

The gist of it is simple. You're very new; this is newer. This is so experimental that before they'll let me take part in it I'll have to sign at least one non–disclosure agreement, and more than one waiver. But they got to me early enough, they say. They can take you away and regrow me. They can give me back to myself.

It'll be slow and painful and it might not work, but if it does, at the end of it, I'll be whole again.

Fully human.

It might not work, but if it does, it'll be the first step toward phasing all of you out entirely.

I should give them a call if I'm interested and they'll set up a time for me to come in for an evaluation. Who? *Them.* It's a cliché, but they really are faceless in this moment, a force of nature rather than anything recognizably human. The intelligent, all–powerful entity that gave me to you. Now they've changed their minds.

At least this time they're asking for my permission.

I don't drink my wine. I put the phone on the table. I put you on the table and I look at you for a while.

This is what I wanted. No learning. No sharing. Just having. No one ever has to know.

Later I go for a run. I jog down the steps of my building and onto the sidewalk, running between pools of light, feeling all of me pumping myself forward. A smoothly–running machine. You working in tandem with the rest of me, so much a piece and a part that there might be no difference at all. But if I feel exhilaration, I can feel that you have your own. My companion. You're coming along with me, and I have no idea if what's inside you is complex enough to make its own decisions or whether I'm engaging in a kind of delusional anthropomorphization, the opposite of the man who removed one leg and ruined another, or if this is really real.

All of it, real. There might be no difference. There might be none.

I don't know if I can do this again. I don't know if it's worth it.

A mile in, you start to hurt me, and I recognize that it's not strain or malfunction but a gentle prodding in the form of an aching throb, you letting me know that you're here. I listen and it's like you're speaking, you're putting in your two cents, whatever they are.

And I think that you didn't choose to be here any more than I did.

And I think that maybe you're just doing the best you can.

And I think maybe all those people who are spending all that time and energy and lying awake nights and writing and writing and talking and worrying and making claims about *what's really human* are sort of full of shit.

I stop and I breathe hard. I lean against a lamp post and you hold me up.

It's their problem. I'm tired of letting them make it mine.

"Let's go home," I say, and I think I can feel you agreeing.

And yeah, maybe this is the wrong decision. Maybe I'll regret it later. Maybe it's my problem after all. Maybe I'm betraying something, maybe I'm not even qualified to make these kinds of choices. Maybe I'm sliding down a slippery slope and maybe I'm shallow. Maybe it's all a delusion, but hey, whatever gets you through the day.

I'm real. So are you. I need you, but I'm not sure I need to be human. I'm not sure any of us is equipped to make that call.

So this is life, now. This is what life is.

I think I can be okay with that.

MEMENTO MORI

||||||||||||||||||||||||||||

"I FOUND THIS. IS IT YOURS?"

It's not mine—I'm already sure about that before I look up, because I know I didn't lose anything. I don't carry much with me to lose and I know it's all here. So whatever it is, I know it isn't mine, but the guy sounds friendly, like he means well, so I look up with my mouth already open to say *No, thanks anyway,* and then I'm face to face with my own skull.

Would you recognize your own skull if you saw it? Would you know the bone structure your own skin has stretched over for as long as you've been alive? Those empty sockets—you've stared out of those sockets for your whole life, and when you've been tired or when you've cried, you've rubbed your fingers against their curves. There's the maxilla, the zygomatic—your cheeks, but it sounds like some kind of fancy new vacuum cleaner or something—lacrimal, nasal, sphenoid. The architecture of your own face. So would you know it, if an old man with a Red Sox cap and a metal detector came up to you on the beach and held it out to you?

I do. I have no idea if that's normal, but I do. So I say, "Yes, thanks." And I take it, and he nods and smiles and walks away, waving his detector over the sand. I've got my skull cradled in my palms—smooth and surprisingly light—and I find myself wondering what else he might find with that thing.

A girl in a blue bikini walks by. She looks at me and I lift a hand and wave, and her face twists with a mixture of confusion and disgust that probably doesn't have a name, and she walks a little faster. It might have been the skull. I want to try to explain to her that it's mine and I can't exactly leave it here on the beach, but I'm pretty sure I would sound like a lunatic, pretty sure she wouldn't believe me. I'm not dressed for the beach, in jeans and sneakers and a baggy t-shirt, and it occurs to me that maybe I should just go somewhere else. I'm not even sure why I came here in the first place.

I mean, I'm glad I did. Someone else might have gotten to my skull before me, taken it from the man, done God knows what with it.

We get up, me and my skull, and I carry it with two fingers hooked into the empty eye sockets. I look down and it looks like it's grinning at me, and I guess pretty much all skulls look like that, but I can see a gold filling in one of the bottom back molars flashing in the sun. That's me. Other people have fillings, sure, but I remember that one, because it was my first one, and I sat there in the creaking leather chair that tilted back and made me feel briefly dizzy under the bright light, and I asked the dentist if maybe he could do it without numbing me up.

It's not that I like pain, you understand. I just kind of wanted to know what I'd be missing.

I head up onto the boardwalk and past the crowds of people getting hot dogs, cotton candy, airbrushed t-shirts, henna tattoos. Maybe I'm not so out of place carrying a skull here, with the skull t-shirts and the skull tattoos and the cheap little plastic skull keychains with eye sockets that light up and flash. You forget that skulls really are *everywhere*, with skin and meat over the top of them as they move and laugh and eat and cry and all those things that living people do.

I cross the street. I walk out into the city, sticky humid and shooting heat up at me from the pavement. I can feel my hands getting slick with sweat. I hold onto my skull a little tighter. I really do not want to drop it. If you drop your skull and it breaks, what does that mean? I know about out-of-body experiences, but this would be something else. This would be looking down at the pieces of me and knowing that they're broken because my fingers slipped. And I wouldn't get to move on—I'd be here, and I'd have to get up tomorrow and live with the knowledge that I shattered my own skull, and there it is, pieces of it being ground into the pavement as people walk over it.

I decide to go to a bar. A man walks into a bar carrying a human skull—sounds like a good setup for a joke. So what's the punchline?

The bar is cool and dim and not very crowded. I like it. There's a rough edge at the place where my nose used to be, the place where the cartilage would meet the bone, and I rub my thumb over it like I'm trying to smooth it out. The man behind the bar—head bald and shining—nods at me as I take a seat.

I put my skull on the bar and he looks at it.

"It's okay," I say. "It's mine." I order a beer and he brings it to me, and he doesn't ask any questions. If he's been doing this job for long enough, could be he's learned when not to ask, and I'm not sure what he would ask me anyway.

The woman sitting to my left leans over. "Is that thing real?" So she has an idea of what to ask, I guess.

I nod and I say it is, and I repeat that it's mine, which seems like an important detail, because it's the main reason I have it at all. If the man on the beach had held out someone else's skull, there's no way I would have taken it. The woman whistles. She has blond hair that looks like it's been bleached fifteen or twenty times, the very color and texture of straw.

"That's really something. Crazy. You just gonna carry it around?"

I shrug. I wish I could explain to her how all of your options dry up and seem pointless next to the smooth, familiar curve of your own cranium in the palm of your hand. That curve swings around and across everything possible in your life, cutting it off like a knife. The longer it stays with me, the less I know what I'm doing.

"Wild," she says, and lifts the glass in front of her to her lips, tosses her head back, and half of whatever had been in it is gone. She does this in an easy, thoughtless way, the kind of way that makes me sure that I'm sitting in the presence of an experienced drinker. I like that, too. I like people who can be professional about whatever it is they do. I tap my fingers on the polished ridge of my brow, and I follow her example and I drink.

I'm not sure how much later it is. I'm not sure how many rounds we've gone through, me and her and my skull watching the both of us with empty sockets. At some point her hand crept onto my knee and I don't push it off, because at this point I don't really feel qualified to turn down whatever else life wants to toss in my direction. I made a choice this morning that seems to have made a lot of other choices easier for me, even as it's made others even more complicated, and on balance that might be good.

I dip a finger into my glass and let a clear drop of beer fall onto the knitted plates at the top of my head. It rolls down to where my ear used to be and pats softly into the table.

"So now there's two of you?" she says, half a question and half just a thing she's saying. I shake my head. This isn't my entire body, I didn't die somewhere else and decompose down to the bone. This is just my skull, and I don't know how it got onto the beach, but it doesn't seem all that important because now we're together.

"Maybe after I'm dead, there'll be two skulls. Then that'll be right, sort of."

She looks at me and nods as if this makes all the sense in the world to her. Then she stands, pulling the straps of her faded sundress up over her shoulders, and she lays a hand on my skull, and there's something kind of proprietary in it but I don't tell her to move it. I don't think she'd try anything bad. We've been talking. She knows how important this is to me.

"Let's get outta here."

I nod, toss some bills onto the bar, pick up my skull and we head for the heavy wooden door, and when we open it and step out onto the sidewalk the sun is going down, the sky hazy and so brightly orange it almost hurts my eyes. Walking isn't a problem, not like if I was drunk—because I'm pretty sure I'm not—but my feet feel like they're not even attached to me, like I'm looking at them from those empty eye sockets, tucked under my own arm, not moving on my own so much as just being carried from place to place. There are people in the street, surging around on foot and in cars, sending noise and exhaust up into the air, but none of it really feels like it has anything to do with me. Beyond the streets and the buildings I can feel the ocean again, like it's tugging on me in that way that every large thing can. I turn my face toward it and I wonder how long my skull was out there. It's so smooth, so clean. How many days and nights did it spend in the sand, tiny grains polishing and polishing?

"You're already thinking about dying?" She startles me when she speaks, and then she surprises me by slipping her arm around mine, my free one. I look at her in the yellow streetlight glow and I wonder how old she is. She looks like she could be any age, though I get the feeling she's older than me. Her skull is a lot closer to the surface, a lot more like her face. "You're too young to be doing that, honey."

I look down again at what I'm carrying. "Kind of hard not to."

"You don't have to take that thing everywhere." She tugs at me, slips her hand into mine and squeezes with her bony fingers, the little knots of her knuckles like tree roots. I'm about to tell her that I do, because it's mine, so what the hell else should I do with it, but she leans up and kisses me just then, just at the corner of my mouth, and her lips are soft and a little sticky with gloss, and for the few seconds she's there I forget about the bones under my skin and the bones under hers, and it's just soft on soft. I almost turn my head. Then I don't.

"Come on," she says, and when she tugs at me again I go with her, and we walk.

Here in the city, it never really gets dark. The places where the darkness is become a little darker, the shadows more sharply defined, but it never *gets dark* in the way that I think people mean when they say that. I feel like we're in a moving spotlight as we head out across the wandering grid of streets, and I don't know whether I'm pulling us or she's pulling us or we're pulling together, or following what's in my hand like some kind of divining rod pulling us toward water.

So we go back to the water. I think neither of us knows that we're going there until all of a sudden, there we are, like we teleported there straight from where we began, beamed down like we're in a science fiction movie. The thing is, I began here at the water, because my skull did. My jawbone is very cool, nestled against my palm.

We stand on the pier. We're the only ones here, and the moon is still low and it's the exact same bleached off-white color of bones. I still don't know the woman's name, I think, but she lets go of my arm and takes my hand, and I let her. It feels good. We look out together at the moon, the reflection of it all broken up on the water's surface like stained glass, and I think about the things they say we used to be, little wormy things with stubby legs that crawled out of the water and up into the trees.

"I used to pretend I was a mermaid," she whispers, and I think, *You used to be one, we all did,* even her with her weird old-young face and her hair like straw, and I still don't know her name, but it still doesn't feel like it matters. We used to be them, but then we died, and our bones are what's left. I never really thought about death before now. It's like they say: it's just this thing that happens to other people. Except it isn't. I'm holding the evidence of that in my hands, something that could have come from the past or the future, or now, right now, because I guess we're all dying the moment we're born.

She lets go of my hand, turns and looks at me. She's swaying just a little, and I guess she might be drunk, but her eyes are so clear, so focused, and I can't look away. She reaches down and rests her fingertips on my skull. I can see her chipped red nail polish shining black in the moonlight.

"You need to get rid of that thing."

I look at her fingers, at the skull, at the way the moon pales her skin into the same color as the bone until they look like they could be all part of the same thing, a mutant on the same order as the wormy things that we used to be, until our shapes changed and we became what we are. I take a slow breath and I move my own fingers up and over the maxilla, zygomatic, lacrimal, nasal, sphenoid. I know it because it's mine, because it's the part of me that my self rides around in and it has been since I was born, since before that. The old man with the metal detector and the Red Sox cap had held it out to me and I'd taken it, because you don't say no to the things that are most completely yours.

But maybe I'm too young to be thinking about death. Or maybe I'm exactly the right age. My fingers touch hers and I think about how her hand had felt in mine, and the softness of the flesh that lies over her mandible and her maxilla.

We all used to be mermaids, until we came up onto the sand. I don't know if that's true, but right now it feels like it could be.

"It won't break," she whispers, and I'm happy that she understands that the issue matters to me. "It'll be just like giving it back, right?"

I guess that's right.

For a few more seconds we just stand there alone on the pier with the waves hitting the pilings in a soft *woosh woosh* and when I feel like I can, I pull away from her and I'm careful, gentle, cradling my skull in my hands like it's something special, something priceless. Because it is, because it's mine, and just because I have two of them doesn't mean it means any less to me.

But really, I think I only need the one. At least for now.

So I wind up like I'm going to throw a football, and I'm conscious of every contracting muscle and every moving joint as I pull back my skull and shove it forward and let it go out into the dark and across that stained glass water. As it goes the moon catches it, frozen in mid-air like another little moon, smaller and dimmer with a face set into it that I know is mine. Then it's gone.

"Okay," she says. "Okay." And she takes my hand again and squeezes it, but she doesn't try to pull me away. I can't see where my skull hit the water. I don't even know that it did. I never heard a splash. It just arced up and over the broken moonlight and then it disappeared in the dark.

I'm not sure why, but I like not knowing for certain. It could be anywhere. Maybe it was never here at all.

Finally I turn around and she turns with me, and we walk again, back into the city, back away from the water, because we came from there but we can't go back there, not yet. Someday. I've got that to think about, and I've got what's under my skin, and right now I've got what's under hers as well. As soon as we get off the pier and back under the streetlights, I'm going to ask her what her name is. And I'm going to say it back to her with each letter getting its own time, shaping each syllable with my face until I can really feel what it's like, because I can feel things. Skulls can't but I can, and that's an important difference, I think.

That I can do that, that's mine, too. And I can't leave it behind.

THE COLD DEATH OF PAPA NOVEMBER

|||||||||||||||||||||||||||||||||||||||||||||||||||||||||||||||||||||

EVERY ONE OF THE LIGHTS OF BUDAPEST IS AN EYE, AND EVERY ONE of those eyes is staring at him. He turns his own eyes to the river, ribbon of darkness cutting through a sea of flying photons, but even the river is not dark; *tilt your head this way and that, laddie, this way and that* and the river looks at him with the reflected gaze of all the lights of the city, his own reflection in the glaze of a dead man's stare.

This way and that. Hands on the old pocked wood of the balcony door. His fingers slide into depressions barely covered by new paint. Head turning, turning. No peace here. Behind him, the shortwave sits on its little table like a gargoyle, glowering at him with its own inscrutable gaze.

Down on the street five stories below, a crowd of people, laughing, happy. *Her* voice for a moment, in the way that all voices are her voice, in the way that all gazes are her gaze. The world is haunted by her.

The shortwave crackles and he tenses as if for a blow, not turning.

Achtung. Achtung. Der Achte. Der Zwei. Der Achte. Der Sechste. Der Drei.

A woman. Not her. His shoulders relax into limpness. He looks out at the city and the city looks back, questioning.

So what did you come here for?

Home, years ago, months ago, hours and minutes; time is more fluid now than it used to be. He marked the passage of time with breaths, heartbeats; he used hers, because she had mattered that much. Then she was gone, and now he's alone with his own rhythms, and they stutter and shake. They seem unreliable. Time slips away. His perception is a sieve and the time passes through.

He takes phone calls, at first—sympathies and commiserations that seem like mockery. He doesn't want to listen, so at last he doesn't. The phone sits off the hook and he and it sit together in silence. There are pictures of her all over the house, looking at him. Her eyes; his own eyes reflected in hers. He used to kiss her with their eyes open. He used to look into her eyes as their mouths slid together, memorizing each gold fleck, each vein of green, irises like unpolished mineral from the secret heart of a stone.

I love you, she whispers into the silent house, the gathering dark and the gathering dust. *What's happening to you?*

He wanders the halls, leans against a wall, slides down to the floor and buries his face in his hands in a vain attempt at sending her away. He wishes he were brave enough to scratch out her eyes.

Love, grief; in a hellish kind of alchemy they transform into hate. The hate turns inward and festers. He is living in a giant wound. He *is* a giant wound.

He sells the house, and says goodbye to no one when he goes. Before he does, he finds himself in the attic, the contents of an old box strewn out all around him, the old shortwave in his lap. He had forgotten it. He's not sure now that he remembers it, holding it in his hands as though he's only seen it before in dreams. The batteries should be dead but it turns on. Dead air. Crackle, shiver, solar breaths, shifting sunspots.

Ready. Ready. Six. One. Two. Five. Eight. Six. Ready. Ready.

The light bulb explodes with a soft *pop*. He sits there in the dark for a very long time after the voice goes silent. He's not ready. He never could be.

||||||||||||||||||||||||||||

Have you ever seen a lassie, a lassie, a lassie? Have you ever seen a lassie? Start looking, asshole.

Seven eight five one six five seven.

You're not ready for anything.

||||||||||||||||||||||||||||

He hears the song in his dreams. Increasingly, he hears it when awake. He first heard it as most people hear such loose bits of the mass culture, something sung by a relative or on a CD of children's songs, or in school. He heard it as a small boy and it stayed with him, wedged into the crevices of subconscious and memory. Then many years later he heard it again, crackling and indistinct, echoing weirdly in the bare-wood emptiness of an attic not yet filled with the detritus of years of occupancy.

She had been sitting curled around the radio, holding it to herself like she was cradling the child she wouldn't ever have. She heard him—a breath, a creaking board, or maybe she just felt the beat of his pulse, the rhythm by which she kept her own time drawing near—and she looked up. Her eyes...that gaze.

Someone else's gaze.

"I'll be right down," she had whispered. The crackling was gone. Somewhere in those moments, breath and heartbeat, she had turned the thing off. "I'll be right down, I'm just, I'm going through some things. Okay?"

Desperation in that last word. He had felt weirdly ashamed, like he had walked in on her masturbating, except that even that wasn't something he felt shame regarding anymore. He had turned, left the attic, and later she hadn't spoken about it and he supposed he had felt that it was for the best.

I can't tell you about what I do, she had said the night he asked her to marry him. *I just can't. Okay?*

Okay. That same okay. Flash in her eyes like that same empty, alien gaze. Later—or earlier, he's no longer sure with how malleable the time has gotten—lying in bed in the dark, an empty patch of cool sheet to his left. Single notes in the night, so soft, the lost echoes of a lost child's music box.

Have you ever seen a lassie. A lassie. A lassie. Have you ever? Seen a lassie?

Go this way and that.

When he walks out of the house for the last time, he has the shortwave under his arm. It's mid-November, and the trees are shaking themselves naked in the rain. He doesn't look back. There are no lights in the windows of the house, and every one is a dead eye. The worst of them, the attic window, he imagines that he might look back at it and see her there, watching him go, her eyes dark holes in her head.

In his imagination—just a dream, never really happened—she opens her mouth and out come the music-box notes, tinny and lost.

If something happens, she had said once, naked and curled around him, *I'll get a message to you somehow.*

Had she been lying?

What are lies? How do you know them when they happen?

Hours later he's on a plane over the Atlantic, looking out at a blessedly eyeless dark—except for his own gaze reflected dimly back to him, and his eyes look empty as the night outside.

Budapest is cold. Budapest is bright. He hadn't expected the brightness. Bright, clear winter days, nights violently lit. He sits in his rented flat on the banks of the Beautiful Blue Danube and wonders if he might have better luck with a cabin in the woods. No one knows him here. Either way he's just as alone. But really, that's not true at all.

He sits on the balcony with the shortwave; he sits on the floor, on the narrow bed; he curls himself around it as he'd seen her do, protective. Except for some clothes and toiletries, it's all he's brought with him. All he has of her. No photos—but she is everywhere. He doesn't need any.

She is everywhere, but here in his arms is still the majority of her. The pulsing little secret at the heart of her life.

Achtung. Achtung. Another woman's voice—a different woman. He closes his eyes against the lights. *Attention: You won't find her here. Not on this station, not in this ether. You could blame the sunspot cycles, the alignment of satellites, the weather, but what it comes down to is that she's gone.*

Der Zwei. Der Drei. Der Ende.

Two days later he's on a plane again, pushing north, voices dancing in the air all around him.

▓▓▓▓▓▓▓▓▓▓▓▓▓▓▓▓

Station change. Little girl's voice, repeating numbers like she's not sure of them, like she's asking a question. *Is this one right? How about this one?* Station change. Single horn blare, piercing, painful; instead of turning it off he turns it up and presses his ear against the little speakers. Moscow is colder than Budapest had been, and Moscow is just as bright. As he moves north, it seems that there is less day and more brightness. Moscow isn't right either. He only stays there for three days and pushes north again. Saint Petersburg is full of night and more full of light than any city he's yet been in, and he cowers in the corner of his sterile hotel room, radio to his ear, listening so hard that he doesn't entirely feel like he's listening with his ears anymore—he's listening with his skin, his cells, the double-helix of his DNA vibrating with sound.

He doesn't even know what he's listening for. He doesn't know how he'd recognize it if he heard it. He's going on faith. If there's a line between faith and desperation, it's a thin one.

It's strange to marry someone and have no idea what they do for a living. Except he knew, or he suspected, and in either case there had been the cover story, the open-air story, and he knew that one, so introducing her at parties had never been awkward. What had been awkward were the long nights alone, the times when she'd vanish for days with no word, the flat, gray afternoons sitting in the silent living room and wondering if this time might be the time when she didn't come back.

After all that, cancer had seemed like such a mundane way to go. It hadn't seemed worthy of her.

So there had been denial, and now denial looks like a thin man with thin hair, lost in a cold-lit night that doesn't even end with the rising of the sun, listening to the chimes and whispers and mad gibbering that aren't meant for him, waiting for the one message that will be.

And it will come. Because none of this makes any sense. In the absence of coherence, he waits for revelation.

It comes with dawn on Saint Petersburg, like the sun is bringing it. He's asleep, and at first it feels like a dream, and it sounds like something out of a dream as well: a crackle, a mutter, a great screaming wall of sound exploding out of the tinny little speakers, grinding and clawing its way into the room. He jerks, rolls, sits up with his eyes wide, too shocked to cover his ears. Later he'll regret it; it's loud enough to hurt, drilling into his brain with the high frequencies, blunt force trauma with the low. It rises and swirls and falls, like wind, like fire, like the agonized wail of things in pain. Not human things. No human ever made this noise.

He breaks the stasis of the shock and lunges for the radio, twisting the dial and turning it down. But not off. He can't lose this. It feels closer than he's yet been, though maybe not to what he wanted. The lights seem fainter and weaker and the shadows in the corners of the room are closing in, putting out their cold fingers and reaching for him. She might be there, in any of them, darkness pouring out of her eyes and mouth.

At the end, her eyes had looked hollow. Like her flesh was already going insubstantial, her bones the only solid things left.

He presses his ear to the moaning thing and listens.

At first there's nothing. Or rather, there's something, but it's more of the same, the rolling screams and mechanical grinding, the sharp twist of feedback. Then, there, under it, flowing beneath the noise like a dark river passing beneath a city. He's groping for it with his brain, slogging through thick sonic mud and trying to reach it before it slips away again. If she's trying to reach him, maybe she has to fight to do so. Maybe she has to fight for that message she promised him.

He's standing in the hall of the old house, staring at the mirror; his eyes are empty pits. Her face is nowhere. There is grinding in the walls.

His face twists with pain; he barely feels it. He's forcing the sound aside like thick curtains, only these curtains are spiked and razor-edged, and they slash at his hands. He's forcing his way upward, up stairs that no longer creak but scream in rage every time his foot lands on them. Up, up past the point at which he might have wished he could stop, but what's carrying him on now is not under his own power.

There's light coming through the cracks in the attic door. Open it; it pours through into his brain.

Ready? Ready, baby? Here it comes. It snaps inside him like an orgasm, like when she'd wrench them out of him with her mouth and her hands. He is conscious of nothing. At some point he opens his eyes; thin morning light streaming in through the windows. He is curled on the floor, the radio lying to the side.

Shattered.

He gropes for it, breath frozen. Not wanting to believe it, even as some part of him feels a heavy pulse of relief, *free*, but it all fades quickly, because of what's under the broken pieces, plastic and wire, scrawled on a torn shred of newspaper.

67.133056 39.666667

"Numbers," he whispers, and laughs for an hour.

After that, he's moving again.

◦◦◦◦◦◦◦◦◦◦◦◦◦◦◦◦◦◦◦◦◦◦◦◦◦◦

The light fades, transmutes into a seemingly never-ending twilight. The lights of Saint Petersburg, of Moscow, of Budapest, they all feel very distant now—and they are, but being and feeling are not always the same. He drives out across a pale country that rolls and swells like a gentle sea, and it lulls him. It's the first thing like peace that he's felt in weeks. The first thing like quiet, but for the rumble of the truck's engine. And there are no eyes here.

There is ice, and the road, and the low, low sun.

He watches the numbers roll on the dashboard GPS, edging toward what he wants. The numbers are like voices, drifting down to him from spinning eyes too far above to see, but they're quiet voices and they only mean to help.

He sees birds, once, a great cloud of them spinning away south over a row of low hills. He watches them—no need to focus too much on such an empty road—their long necks and graceful wings, always pushing up and up, crying to each other. Crying messages. Direction? How do they all know where they should be?

He drives. The snow thickens. Once or twice, he sees low buildings in the distance, but there are no lights and he meets no one. His lips move in the darkening stillness. Old songs like benevolent ghosts.

Have you ever seen a lassie? Go this way. This way.

This is the way. He can feel it pulling at him.

At dawn, he passes into the *zona* without realizing that he's done so. There are no signs, no markings. The place is not identified on any map that he carries, not on any map in the world. He would assume, if he stopped to consider the matter, that there are people who know why to stay away, and people who do not know why, but the avoidance is common to everyone. There are places in the world that scream wrongness, that warn even the birds away. That carry no light.

Yet, he doesn't hear the wrongness when he passes into it. It could be nights of sitting with the shortwave pressed against his ear, so much wrong that now he's deafened to it. It might be none of that. Regardless, what he sees is not wrongness but a vast spread of land, the same as he has everywhere, naked trees and patchy earth blanketed in most places by snow. It's early winter yet but this far north every winter is a hard winter, and now there may be no break in the snow for many months.

Not that he cares. Not that he plans to wait around to see.

What he does notice, if not the wrongness in the very earth, is the quiet. Deeper quiet than before. He hasn't seen people in miles, but life grips even in the emptiest places, and there has always been the feeling of life unseen. Small life. Birds and rodents, rabbits, foxes, secret and strange.

Not here. Nothing here.

Buildings on the horizon. All the roads have been icy but now this road is falling to pieces as well, and he bumps and rattles along, fixing his eye on the squat blocks. Beyond, rising into the bloodless sky, towers like the fingers of a giant's out-spread hand.

He leaves the truck in an empty parking lot, steps out into the snow and starts to walk, head cocked, listening. The buildings rise all around him like thicker trees, empty, windows blasted and glassless, torn curtains flapping in the wind. Even with the wind, such total silence—in a world of people it should be impossible. But this is not a world of people. This is a world without people. They've left their structures and their signs—words he can't even pretend to read, though she would naturally have been able to—but the trees have grown up over their streets, up through their walls and floors, and the snow covers everything. He stops in a clearing that might once have been a park—broken swingset poles like dead tree trunks—and turns, head thrown back and eyes closed, listening. He feels no gaze on him.

He sings. It's a moment or two before he's really aware that he's doing it. *Have you ever? Have you ever?*

This way.

A two-headed bird lands in the snow in front of him, enor-mous and black, its second head shriveled and half-formed on the hulk of its shoulder. It looks at him for a moment or two with its good eyes—a black gaze with no weight behind it, a ghost-look—opens its mouth, and a long grinding scream fills the dead air.

He knows, without having to see any evidence, that she was here.

He knows he won't be leaving.

He sits down in the snow. The bird sits down with him. There are other places like this in the world, he thinks. Pacific atolls, Japanese cities, deserts of melted glass. Known and secret. Hungry place, the *zona*, and what it doesn't kill with fire it kills with slow poison. It pulls into itself, gathering its children. But it still lets them sing in the dark.

He sings, static and the shriek of steel on steel, the scream of breaking atoms. The bird sings with him. Night and the temperature fall together, and the *zona* is hospitable. It won't turn away a weary traveler. And in the shadows, perhaps, she is waiting.

Have you ever? Here.

Now you have.

SO SHARP THAT BLOOD MUST FLOW

▌▌

IN THE END, THE WATER GOES BLACK WITH THE WITCH'S BLOOD.

Before this happens, the little mermaid understands that a deal is a deal, a bargain a bargain, and there can't be reneging. But this isn't reneging, she tells herself as she sinks down, down, down into water so black that in truth it would be difficult to discern witch's blood within it even had a hundred witches been slaughtered in its depths.

She is not sea foam. That was the first lie.

She is also not alive. That was truth.

Being not alive, she has no need to breathe. This is terribly convenient, given what she needs to do next.

▌▌▌▌▌▌▌▌▌▌▌▌▌▌▌▌▌▌▌▌▌▌

Surrounded by a hundred crystal lanterns, a prince dances with his princess. This is iconic, archetypal; many of the people in the assembly sense this on some level and take pleasure in its even perfection. This is the ending of all the stories they have ever been told as children, all the stories they have ever told *their* children, all the stories their children will tell. The prince marries his princess and they dance and are blissfully happy.

She watches them from the parapet, her eyes burning and her feet cut to ribbons by invisible knives.

This was not her ending. And she sees no reason why she should take it gracefully.

The water is dark and deep below her, and she arcs down into it, her gown fluttering around her. She takes particular care to hit the water at such an angle as to break her neck, and so she sinks before she can dissolve on the little waves.

She dies with purpose. This is a truth she makes.

If she were sea foam, she thinks—and perhaps this is after and perhaps it is before or perhaps it is both things simultaneously—she could become the rain and patter down onto his windowpanes, trickle down the glass and watch him inside in his bright warmth. Or in a storm she could come to him riding, or walking, or anywhere unsheltered, and cut down through the air to strike his cheeks. She could fling herself at him and run down his body like sweat, down his face like tears.

She aches with it. It's worse than the knives ever were. The witch never told her that the knives on which she danced would be the lesser pain.

Did she know? She must have. Witches know all the secrets of love; it's what gives them the power to bargain with all its points and angles and gemstone facets.

If she were sea foam. But she is not. Before, she wants it. After, she wonders at what possessed her, but even in the cold heart of the water she still knows.

It takes her a long time to sink, a long time for the deep currents to carry her. Sometimes she thinks she can still hear the music. It works its way into her ears like droppers of poison, and though the cold water denies her rictus, she feels her teeth clench and grind.

As tiny fish nibble on her legs and toes—she still has them, even now, and hates them more every passing second though the knives have at least allowed her a reprieve—she wonders about death, turns the fact of it over in her mind. She is dead, she's sure of that much, but either the witch lied, and that is why she is not foam on the waves—or something else has happened.

Her spirit is not free. And has not passed away.

Perhaps this is what rage does.

She has never felt rage like this, all-consuming, like the coals of deep-sea volcanoes in the core of her breast. She wanted. She reached for. She did everything she should have done. And him.

Him.

But if she's still here, there are other options.

〰〰〰〰〰〰〰〰

She whispers to the current. It still knows her, and carries her corpse to where she wants to be.

It sets her gently down at the mouth of the sea witch's cavern and there she comes to rest against the rocks, the waving fronds of posidonia caressing her limbs. She waits.

"Why have you come back to me?" All at once, without any stirring of the water at her coming, the witch is looming over her, the rags of her twelve tails like surf-beaten kelp, the thin strands of her hair like ancient seaweed. Her eyes are like the coals that burn in the mermaid's heart. "You should be foam on the waves, daughter."

By the witch's magic, the mermaid knows she'll be heard, the voice of that coal as it burns higher and more violent. *I'm no daughter of yours.*

"No. At that, not. So, then." The witch reaches down and lifts the mermaid under the arms, clasps her cold body close to hers, which is hot for a host of dark and unnatural reasons. "This tale has ended badly for you."

You meant it to.

"I meant to exact a price. I would in any case. You must know how these things work. I don't make the rules."

The witch glides backward through the water, back into her cavern, carrying the little mermaid with her. It is an embrace, close and dangerous, not intending comfort, not intending any good, but the mermaid has suffered and is dead and is now not afraid of anything. She has spent some of her time of sinking in wondering what might happen to her now, whether the witch might cut her into pieces and use her disparate parts for her magics, whether she might be skinned and used as a bag or a drifting blanket, whether her muscles and fat might be peeled away and eaten raw, her blood spilling down the witch's chin and floating like red gauze in the little currents.

But now she doesn't think those things will happen. Pressed to the witch's bare, sagging breasts, she can sense the direction of movements. She can see way ahead with her blank, dead eyes.

The witch lays her down in a bed of kelp. The bones of whales hang from the cavern's ceiling and make a soft *clunk* sound when the shifting water brings them into contact with each other. The water itself smells of blood, crushed plants, decay, dark things. The blood might draw sharks, but the rest keeps them away. Keeps everything away but the desperate.

And the dead.

The witch floats above her, arms loose at her sides.

I want to make a deal.

The witch cocks her head on one side. This close, the mermaid sees that tiny, pale shrimp are crawling through the strands of her hair, picking over her scalp. "Another? The way this one has ended? Be serious with me, girl. What could you offer me? And what would you want?"

You know.

The witch is silent for a time. Her fingers wander over the mermaid's body. Perhaps she is learning humanity. Perhaps she has never touched a human woman.

"It would be difficult," she says at last. "It would require much. Heavy magic. Dense and drawn from the core of the world, through the fire towers in the deepest of deeps. And that still leaves open the question of what you could give me in trade. What would be worth so much effort and such a cost to me."

The little mermaid has had an answer for this ready since her body hit the water. She wishes she could smile.

There is one thing. And against all possibility, the corners of her mouth twitch.

Life and strength flow back into the mermaid both together, a great rush like a wave crashing on the shore of her heart.

Her body wrenches itself upward, a great heave, her chest twisting in on itself with the lungs she no longer has. Her legs are bound and blended, her feet splay and stretch into fins. She opens her mouth wide in a scream with no voice to make it heard.

The witch watches her in silence. She was pale before; now her skin is almost translucent. She is exactly the color of the shrimp that infest her hair. She looks as if she's trying to smile but can't, as if she's taken a little of the mermaid's death into herself, because of course she has.

Death always has to go somewhere.

But that leaves the rest of it. The death the mermaid has promised.

The witch places the silver blade into the mermaid's hand. Two seconds later its point is buried in the witch's breast.

This was not part of the deal, not the promised death in trade. But the witch doesn't look particularly shocked as she dies.

The little mermaid sits in the center of the black-gauze witch's blood. It flows into her gills. She opens her mouth and tastes its old metal and rotten wood. What she promised the witch, what she's offered in exchange—she's done offering. Done exchanging.

This is all for her.

IIIIIIIIIIIIIIIIIIIIIIIIIIIIIIIII

She can hear the music of the prince's ship as she nears the surface.

It's music to dance to, and for a moment she stops just beneath the surface, head cocked, listening. She danced once, danced on the blades of knives and never bled, never screamed, and it had not just been that she had no voice. Love silenced her, terrible love, and she only had eyes for him as he laid his hands on her and spun her across the floor. Alone she had danced for his delight, her eyes beseeching him. She had believed he saw and answered her in the same kind. She had believed that he had entered the cloak of silence that covered her. That when his lips touched hers he had shared in it all.

Now she listens, cold as the water around her.

She breaks the surface. The knife is very heavy in her hand.

The ship is strung with fairylights, bathed in starlight. On the deck she can see bodies turning, turning. She can't see the prince or his precious princess, but she can feel him there. Whether or not he meant to, he *did* share himself with her—if, as she now knows, not his better part. Not the part he's given now.

She stabs the blade into the wood of the ship's side and begins to climb.

IIIIIIIIIIIIIIIIIIIIIIIIIIIIIIIII

She knows they won't see her, not at first. They had never seen her, not even *him,* and now will be no different, though she's a thing of legend, of fairytale, as much as the prince and his princess. She's not a thing of *this* fairytale, has no place here, and so will be unseen. She is supposed to be dead. To them, she is.

She can make use of this.

She pulls herself onto the deck behind a table laden with food. Her gills should make this difficult but some part of her remembers, some part of her unable to shed that form just as she can't yet shed all of her death, so the air she pulls into her is harsh, sharp, a little like the knives that used to torment her. Her tail is strong and she uses it to push herself across the deck, behind the guests, behind the men in their fine suits of clothing and the ladies in their rich gowns. Behind the musicians with their strings and pipes and delicate drums.

And there, in the center of the gathering, *him* and *her*.

The mermaid closes her hand on the edge of the shear's blade and bleeds. Because what's a little more blood?

The prince and his princess turn around each other, spinning and laughing, voices high and clear over the music. The mermaid, in spite of herself, briefly loses herself in watching them. They are so lovely in light that dances as they do, fire and stars, and for an instant—a traitorous instant—she wants this again. Wishes. Dreams. Because it might, it *might*, have been worth the pain.

She lets out a sharp hiss.

All at once, the prince and his princess stop, standing in the center of the circle, gaze to gaze, hand in hand, breathless and flushed and so clearly happy.

This is the last scene of the fairytale, the point at which it ends, the book closes, the light goes out and all the good little children snuggle into their covers and drift to sleep on waves of sea foam.

The little mermaid slaps her tail against the deck and *leaps*.

There's silence. She can hear it. The world itself gone frozen and still, and all eyes on her. Her hands hit the prince squarely in the chest, one hand over his heart, and the shock on his face gives her pleasure as keen as any blade that has ever touched her.

From somewhere in the crowd, a scream. The prince himself is opening his mouth to do the same. The little mermaid opens her own in mimicry of him, and before he can utter a sound she plunges her head down and sinks her teeth into his throat.

He convulses under her. His choked-off scream comes out as a gurgle as her teeth dig in and in; hot blood floods her mouth, flesh giving under the force of her bite, and the prince twists, trying to get away, and this is all the help she needs as she whips her head to the side and tears out his throat, meat and voice sweet together on her tongue.

She swallows. The prince lies there, twitching, drowning in his own blood.

Voiceless.

Now the screams, a chorus of them, women and men alike, and the sweetest scream of his princess, but the little mermaid barely hears any of this over the sound of her own laughter, hard and high and like all the songs she used to sing to him unheard beneath the waves. She eats his scream, the blood running down her chin, and as her death flows into the gaping hole in him, his life burns hot in her belly.

Why, he's mouthing. Silent and already half dead. *Why.*

She lowers herself against him and kisses him once, painting his mouth with his own blood, smiling against him, and now understanding that this is a kind of joy he would have never given her willingly. Now there are running feet on the deck, the pounding of fleeing and panicked people, the shouts of the few guards he's brought with him on what should have been a voyage to celebrate life and love. Over the din of all of these things she opens her mouth and speaks to him for the first time.

"Fair's fair," she crows. "Fair is so very fair, and I'll spare you the knives you'd dance on, my love, my love."

She's singing as she begins to cut off his legs with the blade. It is very sharp. The witch gave it magic. He can't scream, of course, as his blood pools on the deck and drips through the slats, but she can feel his cries echoing in her own throat and she turns them into music. To this music, she thinks, she'd dance on knives.

She'd dance and she'd laugh, her teeth glistening like rubies in her mouth.

No one touches her. No one comes near her. She takes the prince's legs in each hand and leaves the knife buried in his heart. She moves to the railing, and before she leaps into the dark she glances back at his princess, still standing at the edge of the crowd, pale as the witch with tears streaming down her face.

Her story has not ended well.

The little mermaid regards her dispassionately, though really, she bears her no malice—the princess has, of course, been allowed to live. In another story the little mermaid knows that it might have been herself. It might have been anyone.

She gives her chin an imperious tilt. The one thing she would never have cared about being was royalty.

"Make your own deals," she says. And lets herself fall.

She slices into the water, a limb in each hand. She lifts the legs to her mouth and kisses each, on the sole of the foot, where the knives had always hurt her most.

And she lets them go.

As she plunges down into the fathoms below, she doesn't look back. The prince's legs float to the surface and bubble, dissolve into sea foam on the waves, and are soon lost and nothing at all.

She allows herself a second to float, light above her and deepest darkness below.

This is a crossroads, a turning-away-forever. But there isn't any going back; that was the deal she made, and she can make her own deals and her own truths, make them solid and real as her flesh will now always be.

TELL ME HOW ALL THIS (AND LOVE TOO) WILL RUIN US

|||||||||||||||||||||||||||||||||||||||||||||||||||||||||||||||||||||||||||||||||||||||||||||||||||

YOU WERE SCREAMING WHEN I PULLED YOU FROM THE BOAT.
You hadn't fallen into a bout of it since we left the mainland.
I'd bound your legs to broken steel poles, kept you as still as I
could, doused you in whiskey. For a time you were quiet while
the sea roared around us. I thought we might die then; I thought
you might die in a kind of peace, and this comforted me when
not much else did. But I made myself ready for my own death
the moment I laid you in the bottom of the boat, and when we
pulled ashore on the long strand, having successfully avoided
the worst of the rocks, I knew it had only been postponed.

Now it's past sunset. I can tell only by the dying light; we sailed
in clear skies but we sailed through storms to reach the island,
and now I think that the storms must always be here, circling the
place, keeping it from the rest of the world. So the clouds hang
heavy here, and it seems appropriate. Looking up the cliffs, the
dark slate, the sparse grass clinging to the ledges and the hillsides, I can't imagine this place under the clarity of full sun This
is a place of darkness and twilight, and in what light dawn allows
us, I'll pull you, no doubt screaming, up the hillside.

I have made a fire from pieces of driftwood. It smells like
salt and wet sand, and it smokes badly. You lie wrapped in the
blankets I bought. With the aid of more whiskey, you sleep. I
sit in the cold, unprotected, and I think of you and what might
come after. How much of this will you remember? Enough to

be grateful? Enough to know that I loved you? That for a while, maybe, you loved me?

I will show you, in the most vicious way that anyone can. You may be lucid. This is another thing I've given up caring about, because there's only so much I can afford now.

※

I remember when you took me.

We all do, those given to the rest of you to be your hand-maidens, to be kept by you. The rest of you who keep the world turning, who bring up the sun and the moon and who, as in the stories of the elder days, bring us the rich harvest. All that power, closed up inside you. We're never told why you begin too weak to free it on your own, why you need us to do it for you. But anyway: You were singing as you stepped up to me and I handed you my sprig of blackthorn and meadowsweet. You were singing as you kissed me and I knew I would never leave you until you needed me to.

You'll sing to me now. Sing me up the terraces, over the abandoned pastures. Sing the slip and slide of gravel under my feet but don't let me fall. Sing me through the strings of barbed wire, play on it with the wind like a cello. I'm in pain but it's nothing to yours, I'm terrified but it must be nothing to your terror, but you have the power in this equation; only lend me a little. Just enough.

I was never a witch. So sing the magic into me. Soon I'll sing it back to you. We'll make a duet of flesh and blood and bone.

※

It's not as though you did magic, not that I remember. We're taught from a young age that the magic is inside of you, locked into a chrysalis, waiting to emerge. We are the kept ones. We are the knife that cuts through and sets it free. We don't understand how, or when. We're ready, every minute of every day. Of course this isn't true. Of course, at the precise moment for which we've always prepared, there is mad panic.

I have a knife. It's stuffed into the side of my boot. I can feel it against me like a brace, like a smaller version of what's holding you together now that I can't anymore. I have a knife, which is not yours but which was instead given to me by the old woman in the shack by the sea, the one I found, wandering away from the rocks and screaming your name for lack of anything else to do. When I was sure you were dying. When I knew you were. I found her by her fire and she told me what to do.

She gave us the broken steel. She said it had been split by lightning. We bound your shattered bones in ruin. She summoned me, and you did through her. Perhaps she was waiting, and perhaps she was the first tentative emergence, called into being by you for this specific purpose.

I'm not like you. This doesn't belong to me. But I promise to try.

IIIIIIIIIIIIIIIIIIIIIIIIII

You never liked me to come into the bathroom when you were there, but on that rainy Sunday I did anyway, drawn by your voice and the splash of the water. I sat on the toilet and looked at you as you covered yourself in bubbles, laughed at me. Your slick thighs. Your nipples just visible under the water, brown and relaxed in the heat. The tile beaded with condensation. You hadn't called me, you were reading poetry aloud to yourself. I asked you to read to me. I only had to push a little, and you went through all the lines. You read me more than I ever asked for. In the end: you, head tipped back in the water and your hair glossy black like a seal, crying. Your tears dissolved in the tub and I thought of you making a tiny ocean through will alone.

I could read poetry to you now. I didn't bring any books, but I remember your favorites, I can read them from the book of us that lives under my skin. Your head is in my lap, and I can give thanks for this much: you're warm. You will stay warm. I'll keep you that way. I'll love you and keep you, which I promised to do, and in the end I forgive you. For the choice I made when there were no alternatives.

||||||||||||||||||||||||||||||

We could go anywhere, I said. You picked the place. I knew you for ten years before you fell, and you were always running away from something. Never me, at least I don't think so, and I base this last of my few remaining convictions on the fact that when you made that final lunge for a world without anyone else, that world included me. We called it a vacation. You were happy. Maybe some part of me knew then. We parked the car on the edge of one of the cliffs, a barely-paved road winding like a lost ribbon against the top, and you looked out at the ocean and yelled and threw your arms around my neck, tangled your fingers in my hair, kissed me and kissed me.

It was sunny that day. I remember. Other things have faded into insignificance, even my early memories of you, but I do remember that. The last happiness before the step, the slip—was it a slip? Did you fall?

Did you jump?

The last of you is a litany of screaming. It's how you mark your time. Strength to scream and then strength gone and gathered to scream again. At first I thought about smashing your head in with a rock to stop your agony. I'm ashamed of it now. But seeing you dead felt preferable to seeing you in pain that way, broken on the rocks, regardless of the choice that put you there.

Your white bones, splintered and stabbed through your skin. Your blood. Your mangled flesh. The way you went pale. I saw you begin to fade out of the world. I held you against me and you just kept screaming.

My pants and hands are painted with your blood. At the darkest point of the night I lift my fingers to my mouth, copper and grit, and lick them clean.

***

Dawn. I haven't slept. You have, though I don't know if the thing you've done could be properly called sleep. But you're awake as I get to my feet, as I look down at you you're looking back up at me, and for the first time since you fell your eyes are clear.

I wait for you to speak, but of course, you don't.

I have to do this, I say. I have to. You know that, you did this. You don't nod. You don't give me any indication that you understand me but I know you do and for a horrible moment I'm angry at you, because this is so hard on me already and you're doing nothing to make it any easier.

As soon as there was light I made a sledge for you out of more driftwood and rope from the boat. It may not hold together but then again it might, and there's nothing else. I'm gritting my teeth as I try to lift you just enough to get you onto it; you're a dead weight, not helping me but not fighting, which I suppose I can be grateful for, and also, that you aren't screaming. Maybe you've moved into a place beyond pain.

I have to hurry.

I take the ropes of the thing, loop them around my arms, and start to plod up toward the least steep incline of the hill. It's still steep, sliding rock and loose grass, and if I fall too, there won't be anything left, but like I told you: Choices. That I make, when all others are removed. That you put me in the position of making. I don't know that any of you really trust us when we're given to you. We're given these horrible options, we're pushed by you into jumping.

There was no stone shack. There was no fire, no bent old woman in a fog bank. There was no wind chime of rib bones, there was no blood, no cold spells. There was a boat and there is an island but we would have come to those things by other ways, other means. Or we wouldn't have, and it would have been you on the rocks and me beating myself into the surf, but anyway: there was no shack, no woman, no magic. Not absent you.

It was the first emergence, light through the veins. You tore a hole in time and placed yourself on the other end of the rip. You were ancient in that hut and maybe you didn't expect me to recognize you, but I did.

She walked with a limp.

The island proceeds upward in stages, terraces, things that looked carved with intent. My back is aching as we continue, my arms, and it begins to feel as though, while your bones were broken at once in a terrible series of seconds, mine are breaking slowly over long hours. I pull you and I pull you, dead weight behind me, pausing every hour to make sure that you aren't, in fact, dead. I have a watch, solar powered, and it still works in spite of the lack of sun. Without the sound of your agony I mark the time that way.

I can see the stones now. They're still so distant, protruding from the top of the island, like a crown, like blunted teeth. They'll gnaw at me. I'll feed myself to them and pray that I'm enough meat for what I need them to do.

I think it's midday. I have no way of knowing for sure. As I said, it's true that I have my watch, and I can detect the sun moving through the fog and cloud-banks, but time here is so strange, unreliable, and seems to skip about as if delighting in its freedom from human-constructed tracking devices. It certainly cares nothing for what I'm trying to do.

Anyway: You start to sing.

At first I think it's only the wind, barreling its way up the line of the cliffs, passing like a rough hand over us as I drag the sledge up the series of terraces. I'm now sure that they were formed by human hands at some point in the very distant past, and my way is marked by laid stones and rotting logs, the remains of walls. Divisions of the land. But now there's no one to maintain them; this place has not belonged to people for centuries, and the thought of your voice absent pain is strange to me. So you sing, and I don't recognize it for what it is, except that I find myself singing along. Songs we used to share, in front of fires and streetlights on river water, songs we sang in bed. You were full of them to overflowing.

I sing and I know the song. When I know that it's your voice beside mine the world blurs away, but I continue. In weariness and terror so great that it feels as though it exists outside of and surrounds me rather than originating in any kind of interior state, I find that I have forgotten the words. But I make sounds like words, things that are the worn remains of words. I look at the standing stones in the distance, their pale weathered faces, and I send my word-ruins up to them. Then I fall silent and only your voice remains, low and somehow strong in spite of everything.

There is no moon in the sky and then there is, sister to the sun and holding close. I'm unsurprised to see it; you put it there to give additional light to guide me by. You've never called the moon before but I know it for what it is.

As for the stones, they may know their own when we reach them. The old woman said they might open themselves to us, part as a gate to a way. She said the world you made might be merciful. Then she laughed and laughed.

⁓⁓⁓⁓⁓

Night again. It comes on fast, like the fall of a dying hand. I don't make a fire. I sit on a clear patch of ground, mostly exposed slate, and it's cold but I wrap myself around you, as best I can without touching your broken legs. I checked the wrappings before the light died, and I saw blood blooming up through the cloth. I have no idea if you're dreaming. What would you dream of, if you did? The last inches of thin air between you and the rocks? The taste of my mouth? The crash of the waves?

Or would you do what you will do, with my knife, and dream the world into being?

I hope you do. Before the meager light returns we'll make the final ascent, and there must be something left here for you to return to.

⁓⁓⁓⁓⁓

The wind should be at its cruelest here. Instead it has died, and everything is silent. No waves crashing against the rocks below. No creak and grate of wire. No whispering of grass. No singing, yours or mine, and you seemed to have screamed out your pain long ago. Even the sound of my breathing is dampened. The scratching slide of the sledge over the gravel. Nothing.

The light rises over the circle of stones. It rises out of them. It's my beacon. I follow it on breaking legs, my head full of rocks and crashing surf. But silent.

Should I make my own little bloodless magic? In the silence that remains, should I give you poetry that made you cry?

We never wrote our own. We were always stealing meaning

from everywhere else. You'll steal from me, except I don't think you could steal what's freely given.

‖‖‖‖‖‖‖‖‖‖‖‖‖‖‖‖‖‖

So we come to the stones.

They aren't very tall. I don't know what I expected, I don't know why they loomed so large on the lower hillsides, except that they're clearly the only part of this place that's lasting and real, and I can feel what they can do. What you can do within them. I drag you into their center and let the ropes slither down my arms like seaweed, and I turn to you. As before your eyes are open and they bore into mine. Cut, like a knife. You know. You're lucid. And you're utterly without mercy.

Here there's light, more than anywhere else. Here there's wind, soft and dull, but it moans through the stones, almost inaudible, your voice. And here are the things that keep me here, staring at you, reaching into my boot for the knife.

You: singing love songs on the balcony of that first hotel, your hands wet with sweat of a champagne flute and your fingers on my cheeks. You: running on uneven pavement in new shoes and almost falling until I caught you, laughing. You: lighting fingers calling a storm. You: lips against my ear telling me how all this was going to work. You: shattered on the rocks with your hair a slick, wet tangle, staring up at me, pleading, yes, but behind the weakness a certainty that this was a final test of your power. My love.

And the knife and the fire and the stone.

The first cut doesn't hurt; I'm faintly surprised. Kneeling before the central stone, thick and gray and wearing a coat of dully-colored moss, the blade of the knife parting the skin of my upper thigh, it should hurt. It should be agony. Blood runs down and makes dark patches in the dirt, and I cut deeper, flaying back the flesh, red and pink and the pale yellow of fat. I catch a glimpse of bone. With bizarre, clear precision I avoid the artery; I must be conscious. I must stay alive until the end.

And still no pain. I don't look up at you, I can't, I don't know if I could go on if I did, but I wonder if you're eating the pain, pulling it into you to become poetry later on, murmured out over your flesh remade. You're stronger than me, love. I need you to be.

My skin comes away in thick strips. The blood makes the knife slippery. Twice I nearly drop it. I lift one of my hands and paint the side of the stone, turning the moss black. And here comes the pain at last, perhaps more than you could take, crashing against my rocks. Hissing through my grass. Almost pushing me over. But I love you. I keep cutting. And now here are my bones, here is my exposed hillside, my cliffs. Here is what I can break myself against. For you. All for you.

I pile my flesh at the foot of the stone, under my bloody hand-prints. I lay my skin over it like a sheet. There's a heavy rock by the stone, because there had to be. I don't know if I'm strong enough, except I know I will be because you will it so. My final ascent. My final fall. I pick up the rock; with it in my hands at last I can lift my gaze to yours. And of course your lips are moving. You, crying like before, burning with life, and if you were in the water you would be making it boil.

I don't hear my own bones shatter. I hear your voice, strong and beautiful as you unmake the world.

We tell a story of one of us who died—how does not matter—and who was laid out at her keeper's side. Her keeper was still asleep, dreaming of wholeness, but she was awake and watching before the darkness took her. She spoke to them before that happened, and she said in the end you decide why you're alive and that determines how you die.

She died in silence with her eyes open.

Her keeper sang contralto at her funeral, left pages of poetry on her casket in lieu of flowers. In the end she went away, thinking that, while it wasn't a good ending, it had at least been one chosen.

In a manner of speaking.

LOVE IN THE TIME OF VIVISECTION

||||||||||||||||||||||||||||||||||||||||||||||||||||||||||||||

OVERVIEW

I'M ASKING QUESTIONS WHEN HE MAKES THE FIRST INCISION. THIS is the deal we made.

Why?

Why is always there. You can come at it in a number of different ways.

You can ask at the beginning, when the cuts are small and fine and the pain is keen, or somewhere in the middle when the pain lessens and you begin to be able to feel your muscles divided and peeled back and away from your bones, or toward the end, when the pain is gone and he has his fingers in the slippery tangle of your viscera. When he holds your heart in his hands.

You can be direct, blunt, or you can be subtle and careful and lead up to it with all kinds of nuances and implications; you can create a lovely garden labyrinth of words and at the center of it is the question. Whose way out does it represent?

Who escapes?

This is another question. You must never ask this one. Both of you will fear an answer.

||||||||||||||||||||||||||

ONE

I ask *why?* I am very direct by nature. He meets my eyes as he peels back the skin over my ribcage. There is a little blood but not very much. This is taken care of early on, by means that are unimportant to the greater inquiry. I will not bleed to death. I will not bleed at all.

Why? And he gives me reasons. There is a very long list. I will give you a few of them: *Because I have to, because it's time, because it's what you wanted, because I love you.*

These reasons may or may not be legitimate. The deal we made does not require that he answer me honestly.

A SETTING

Stripped of its skin, muscle is very beautiful.

He brings a mirror and shows mine to me, my powerful, corded thighs and the harder stripes of red and white at my hips and the bars of my stomach. My arms. He has left my breasts untouched; those will be handled with exquisite care when most of the rest of me is done. I am a creature of glistening red. I am a wet ruby, run through with pale flaws. I move—I still can, a little—and I watch my gemstone body pull and flex.

He says he loves every part of me. As he pulls me slowly to pieces, he has an opportunity to acquaint himself with all of those component parts. This is both a gift that I give to him and a demonstration of himself to me, proof of what he says.

The ultimate test of any claim is whether one can hold to it when it is made as literal as possible. As literal as flesh. As bone. As the edge of a knife.

ANNIVERSARY

We made this deal years ago. We sealed it with words but deals like this must always be sealed with much more. I wore white, he wore black; we balanced each other. But all balances are a kind of lie, covered over, possessing buried seeds of conflict. This does not necessarily mean fighting, but it does mean that in the end someone will be cutting and someone will be cut.

I remember how my hand fitted into his. I remember: I knew then that his hands would tear me to pieces. And that I would allow this.

TWO

What does this make you feel? When he finally does carve my breasts away, they tremble. As if they're afraid of him. As if they ache for him. And I am still in pain, gentle pain that washes over me like warm waves. But my breasts are not the question. I am not the question. He is. *Answer yourself. What are you feeling right now, with me in your hands?*

If you wish, you can lie. If you really believe that will save you.

UNFORESEEN CONSEQUENCES

I also promised years ago that I would never hide anything from you.

Now I am being tested, too.

THREE

I lose my muscle. Before, I could barely move; now I am immobile, stretched out flat with nothing to shift my bones. He brings silver pans and pails and lays the strips of me carefully into them. My skin is stretched out on a rack; it already looks like leather. He could wear it, if he chose. He could play at being me. He could wrap it around himself like a cloak. I would shelter him.

But I do not think he would understand me any better.

Don't believe the old stories. Love is the opposite of understanding. When we understand, love is no longer possible.

I ask my third question as the pain fades. *What will you do?* When I am finally pulled apart and all he has are the pieces of me, and those make very poor companions. *What will you do then?*

I don't know.

I cannot be sure, but this feels like truth.

SENSE MEMORY

Once: He is looking into my eyes. We lie face-to-face, skin-to-skin, but the skin feels like a barrier. His lips brush my ear and he whispers that he would like to remove it someday.

Once: It was a kind of play. At any rate, I believe that he believed it was so.

COMMUNICATION

He hasn't touched my head. I still have my skin, my muscles; I can augment my words with expressions. He can see what I feel as it twists at my mouth. I have my eyes and ears; when sensation vanishes I will know that my body is being separated from me.

He will leave my head until the end. This is so he will be able to say goodbye.

THE FINE PRINT

At some point in this process you may wish to renege. The terms may no longer appeal.

This will be impossible. The moment you begin you've already gone too far to turn back.

FOUR

While he removes my guts, I consider my fourth question. I must choose carefully, I must be very deliberate about my phrasing, but it's hard to focus when he lifts my liver out of my body cavity and gently inserts the blade into it. It's like watching him cut into a fruit, soft and overripe, exotic and dark and rich. Something that has sat for a time in its own juices, in the sun.

There is one question I want to ask. But then, it's not really even a question. It's a request, and requests are not covered under the terms of the contract. I cannot make them, and he is under no obligation to acknowledge them should I do so. And how would he punish me for the violation?

Perhaps by refusing to continue.

But we both know that will not happen.

Will you stop?

It could be a question. It could be at the center of my cool green labyrinth, but within that hidden center it could change its shape the instant it's found, like a camouflaged predator. *Will you stop? Will you?*

Please.

I ask it, my changeling question. I wait to see if he will accept it as his own.

But of course I already know. Whether it's a question or a request, there is only one possible answer to either.

SECONDS OF SHARPENED FLINT

The removal of my heart should be a sacred moment. A sacrificial moment. It should be an offering of something. But it's lost in a mountain of offerings. It is set apart by nothing but my feeling that it should be somehow different than everything else.

In this moment I begin to understand that when everything is drenched in holiness, everything becomes profane.

WHAT REMAINS OF ELEPHANTS

He does not stop. He undresses me down to the bones and I lie there with my head intact and he lifts it to show myself to me, his fingers gentle against the nape of my neck. He has stripped away the last of the flesh, left the ligaments for now but polished me with rough cloths and oils. I gleam. I was a gem; now I am lovely carved ivory, pale and perfect. Except for my head, flesh and skin and muscle and hair; this part of me no longer fits what is left of my body. I have not yet been dismembered but I am already incongruous. I do not connect.

He begins to cut the ligaments away. He is so careful with the cartilage, not to nick or scratch the bone. He wants to keep me perfect until the very last. I appreciate this kind of care.

It is now the only kind he can give me.

THESEUS IN REVERSE

I am a garden. He has pruned me. This is one other way to the center: You can follow the path of the labyrinth or you can take up your blade and cut your way straight through.

〰〰〰〰〰〰〰〰〰

FIVE; A LEAVETAKING

He takes my bones away one by one. He holds them in his hands and runs his fingertips over the lines of them. He is meditating on the subject of me. He lays them together in a gilded basket and then I am just a head, staring up at him, breathless and bloodless but still here. I am reduced. I am made essential.

I ask my final question.

Will you do this again?

This is a question that is also goodbye, because of what it makes implicit. I am passing away; he may someday take another to replace me, and then he will—again—have to decide what to do.

For a long time we merely look at each other. I love him; he must be able to see it. And I know that he loves me, because that was the entire point of this exercise.

He bends to kiss me, so light. And then his answer is the blade through my skull and into my frontal lobe, and *goodbye* is made final.

He will do it again. Over and over and over.

BENEDICTION

My one remaining hope, as I become an artifact of his extremely fickle memory, is that someday he will find someone stronger; strong enough to make a very different kind of deal.

A SHADOW ON THE SKY

|||||||||||||||||||||||||||||||||||||||||||||

WE FOUND HER ON THE THIRD DAY, SPINNING WHIRLWINDS AROUND her fingertips.

You must understand that this may or may not have been true, they may or may not have been whirlwinds, and she may or may not have had death in the ichor of her eyes and knitted into her skin, and she may or may not have looked into our hearts, passed judgment, rendered a verdict and delivered our sentence.

She may or may not have done those things, but we know what we saw.

Given that I am the only one who has returned to tell the tale, you will have to make up your own mind whether or not to believe me.

||||||||||||||||||||||||

As for me, those three days before, they found me in the coffeehouse and laid two hands on my shoulders, spinning me around so that my cigarette almost fell from between my fingers. I was annoyed and I did not hide it. They didn't care and they did not hide that either, two large men with stern expressions and very blue eyes. Foreigners, and not military, or at least I was reasonably certain of that. We know military men by now-yes, something specifically about the men. We know them intimately.

I shrugged before they began speaking, my whole aspect carefully crafted disinterest. But then they told me what they were willing to pay.

"You understand there will be a higher price," I said. "No one finds her and escapes unscathed." They nodded, and I shrugged again. Perhaps they wondered why I didn't seem afraid. Here, I will tell you: None of us are afraid of her because we know her and at the same time we do not know her, and we have long since accepted everything she is.

And also we ceased to fear death a very long time ago. This is what fifty years of death from the sky does to you. Yes, half a century; we are locked in place and in time by what has been done to us and they are locked in place and in time by the tools they use to make us die.

I said I would take them to her. I realized later, as we crossed the desert, that I had been waiting to be asked to do it for a long time. I did not believe that she would leave me alive, just as a storm sweeps away everything in its path. I never expected to return. So really, the money was incidental at best. I had no dependents, no children, no husband. I had no one to leave it to. I had no reason to accept it as an inducement to risk my life.

Clearly I had other reasons. They are none of your business. I don't tell everything to everyone.

We tell stories of her. These are nighttime stories, tales told in the dark, many times to children, because frightened children grow up to not be frightened, or so we say. But not as a threat, not to make them behave. Once we said *go to sleep or I will call your father,* and then we said *go to sleep or I will call the plane,* and then we said nothing because there was nothing left to say, but then there was her and now we tell stories again because she gave them back to us. I will never tell these stories to my children, for as I said, I have none and now likely never will, but it satisfies me that they will be told.

Our queen of the death machines, queen of the desert sands. Queen of piercing sight and hellfire. In a sense she is our patron. In a sense she is nothing like us at all.

They shouldn't want to find her. In a hundred years they have learned nothing.

⸺⸺⸺⸺⸺⸺⸺

They perceived the desert through the night-vision goggles I gave them, old, rubber brittle and flaking away but still functional in the way that all necessary things are made to be. I had my own set, of course, and as we began walking through the dark all of us saw a flat darkness horizontally bisected by a lighter green. And out of that last there were brilliant green lines piercing downward through the air and seeming to penetrate the ground. They shifted, moved, bars of shimmering emerald. They may have been death and they may have merely been eyes that ever watched; long ago we stopped drawing distinctions between the two and longer still we accepted them as a feature of our brave new world.

Is it like this where you come from? I thought but did not ask. *Is your night run through by the light of God?*

The first time I saw those moving beams of green, I felt awe. It was the first awe I had ever felt, and I didn't like the sensation. That time, I tried to take off the goggles, but my mother held them to my face. *You must see,* she hissed into my ear, hand on my trembling shoulder. *You must see and know.*

We stole between them, black shapes rampant on a green field. This is a skill we now all possess, the ones left alive.

⸺⸺⸺⸺⸺⸺⸺

At dawn we made our fire and they asked me for my stories. They were paying me well, so I gave them. And I was in a state of expected death, so I decided that someone at least should have a chance of carrying them back. If either of them survived as well.

In the old days she was the daughter of a distant village, I said. Her beauty was legend, and in addition she was full of virtue, kind and honest. She had many suitors but gently rejected them all, and was permitted to do so by her good father, whose standards were just as high as hers.

And then one day the planes came, and there was no more village. Only her, blood-covered and burned, standing in the wreckage.

God spared her for a purpose and when she cried out to Him in her suffering and her rage He reached down His hand and delivered to her a new tongue. So she called to the planes and they answered, transmissions interrupted and programming rewritten, recognizing a new master. The death machines made new death and she drove the aliens from the desert, reclaiming the craters and jagged rocks and dry brush as hers and hers alone, for her heart is the heart of the death machines and no longer has room for any other.

No one writes these stories down. No one needs to. They are no sacred book, no word of God delivered by an angelic voice, but they are ours and we keep them close.

"You have this one now," I said. "Learn what you can. Stories are maps to what is."

Though I don't expect that it will save them. Not that it ever saves any of us. Not from the planes. And now not from her.

<hr />

We had heard them in the town, that distant buzzing; we always hear it now, though we rarely see. Another story that we tell is one of constant terror, of children living in fear so pervasive and so piercing that it rendered them numb, an entire generation with that part of themselves worn away. They are us and we feel that numbness. We sit on the roofs of our houses and in cafes and we never look up anymore. I don't remember a time without the planes, though I was told yet more stories about those times, like legends from long ago. They were as believable as legends, and even so young, curled against my father's broad chest, I never accepted them as the truth. But I saw the two of them with half their gaze fixed on the sky, never moving, looking for the source of that buzz, the eye from which it came, and I tried not to smile.

Oh, you will never understand. You who sent them to us.

But here in the desert the buzzing is louder, lower, and sometimes we see shifting shadows close to the sun, and then in the dark we see those moving shafts of green light. Their targeting systems are always on, whether or not they are meant to be made imminent use of. The thing, I said to the two, as I told them my stories, is that now we are in *her* land, where her machines fight your machines, and we can never be sure who is watching us. They have many eyes, I said. Hundreds of eyes in one machine. I think of burning angels with many eyes and many wings, stories told to me as a child when I was still afraid of everything. But these machines are possessed of no divinity that we recognize. They are heavenly fire but we are all forever doubtful of their right to pass judgment on us. Not that the right to do any such thing matters. I saw my mother and father judged by the planes. I saw them torn to pieces by a wave of heat and flame, standing in the center of a crowded market, as I turned back to ask them if I could buy a bag of candied dates. I was thirteen years old, a child, but no one can truly be a child here, and I was old enough to know that whatever judgment had fallen on them, it was not justice.

And it made no difference.

I said, God has not saved us. God has not reclaimed His skies. Unless you consider her.

And then, very far above, there was that explosion of fire. The two of them let out cries in unison, awe and fear, as the fire expanded. I watched impassively. "They are fighting," I said, and pointed. "The fight is over. One of them has died. Her machines have taken one of yours. One less beast of the air."

"How do you know?" They stared at me, their eyes like great moons. "How do you know who won?"

I flashed my teeth. I am a beast, too. "I know."

The flat lands became hills all around us. Our water ran low, but I assured them that before long we would encounter a spring, the spring of Hasadat, which I did not translate, because of course they knew only the basics of the language of the land into which they strode. They were weary but they didn't complain and I suppose I gave them a kind of credit for that. But they were also more and more afraid, looking around at the shadows and falls of the hillsides, the jagged crags where parts have fallen away, as if they expected attack to come from them. Though of course no attack that we should fear will come from the ground.

"Why do you want to find her?" I asked that night. It was my turn to demand stories. "What do you hope to gain?"

For a long time they both sat in silence. I didn't care, especially, but if they were to die I had a vague interest in understanding what they thought they were dying for. Even if they didn't believe they would die at all.

"We wanted to see," one of them said finally, simply. He sounded almost surprised, as if he couldn't quite understand it himself, as if he was only now trying to find the words. "We heard so much, we saw the footage everywhere, and then we didn't see the footage anymore. They talk about her as if she was a lie. So we wanted to see."

I nodded. Then I said, "There once was a story of a

jackal-headed god who weighed the hearts of all the dead against a feather. If the hearts were heavy, he fed them to a great crocodile and that was the end of them. No Hell. Only oblivion." I cocked my head, my eyes narrowed. I supposed these people were interesting after all, after a fashion. "Do you want to know the weight of your hearts?"

They didn't answer. My own heart was a crocodile's grin and I knew it was heavy enough. We are all born knowing what our ends will be. One does not live under the singing of the planes with a heart lighter than a feather.

Plodding induces meditation—and that far into the journey, we no longer walked. We *plodded*. Plod. The English word—I appreciate the way it sounds, like the thing being done. Heavy and ungraceful. Vaguely useless. We plodded along and I thought, *What is money? Why am I taking theirs?* Was it some kind of reflexive action? Does that kind of exchange become second nature? I knew I had other reasons, but they were still mysterious to me.

What kind of creatures are we now? Beasts, acting without thought?

They would not even live long enough to pay me. Surely not. And I would not live long enough to spend their pay even if they did. I laughed to myself; they would perhaps give me the money and then in the seconds between it leaving their hands and entering mine she would judge and feed us to her machines.

Surely they could not escape that fate.

But even we who have lived in two shadows for so long do not understand her. We don't know her thoughts. I could not hope to guess, as if my guesses meant anything at all.

I prayed to her, at last. This feels like a confession, because I was raised to believe it was a sin. A messenger of God, a demon—both of these things are true. But I prayed to her, my forehead in the dust. I did not ask for forgiveness or mercy; I knew she had none of either for any of us. I did not ask for favor, or a sign. I did not ask her to rise up and smite our enemies with hellfire. I did not ask her for anything.

I said what so many before me have said, what was said at the beginning of everything. The one thing that all of us can say without reservation.

Except even that might no longer be true.

I am here.

She cannot be invoked. She does not come when called.

But she came.

||||||||||||||||||||||||||||

The green lines expanded and covered the ground. They blinded us all; we swore and pulled off the goggles, but the light was still there, massive, like blows to the brain, and none of us could hide.

Light of God. I laughed and spread my hands, lifted them to the sky. Behind me, *they* were screaming, and I took no particular pleasure in their terror. It was merely a thing that was true and that had to be, that was always going to be so, and now that it was happening I felt a sense of relief.

Listen: I have a secret to tell that is not a secret at all. From the moment we are born and we begin to hear stories of her, from the moment we can understand their meaning, all of us want to be taken by her, a little. As if it were a kind of salvation. As if she had the power to send us to Paradise, though of course our hearts are all far too heavy. It does not matter—she is filled with the wrath of God, and even His wrath is beautiful.

And so she was beautiful.

She stood there, barely a hundred yards from us, her arms

raised as if she meant to embrace us. Rags whipped around her body and her head, and through the few gaps that remained in her blinding light I saw—with bizarre clarity—her scarred face, her hollow cheeks, her eyes that burned green hellfire. Her mouth open and singing.

Ayah. A gasp. A gift.

The death machines screamed and descended and came among us.

I saw them, in the few seconds before they seized my heart. They were all shapes and no shape at all. They were like gun-metal-gray birds without eyes, with eyes in their bellies, with eyes all over their skin. Their rotors beat the air into submission. Small ones swarmed. The great ones hovered, jets blasting the sand away. They knocked us to the ground and there was only light.

I glimpsed the people I had brought there, lying a few feet away from me. They looked as if they were already dead, eyes wide and staring, jaws slack. I tried to scream to them. I tried to say, *This is what you wanted. This is what you have done.*

Her hands were on me. I arched into her, laughing as she cut out my heart with her green beams.

And there is not much else to tell. I never saw the bodies of my companions. They were utterly destroyed, as must be when a heart is too heavy—nothing can remain. The earth must be swept clean, all sign removed. This is to restore a balance, to wash all refuse away, as it was when God sent the flood that bore Nuh and his family into a new world.

This is her work.

As for me, clearly I was not destroyed, which surprised me. Because there is a part of the story that none of us tell. No one has ever returned to tell it. I am the first. I have chosen this, because stories should be told, and I want the world to know her as I know her now. To worship her as I have done. To understand what it will mean when at last she comes for you all.

There was a home for my heavy heart. She made one. She gave me eyes and wings and the sky, and the light. Now I am very high, so high that no one can see me, but I see you. I see so much.

There is hellfire in my hands.

Perhaps it will be today, when she gives the command. Perhaps tomorrow. Perhaps a year from now. But until she does, I and my brothers and sisters will be waiting, circling like vultures, and we will be ready.

You will hear us singing before the end.

IT IS HEALING, IT IS NEVER WHOLE

||||||||||||||||||||||||||||||||||||||||||||||||||||||||||||||||||||

WHEN THE SOULS OF THE SUICIDES COME TUMBLING OUT OF THE LOW, gray clouds, it's given to us to collect them, catalog them, contain them, and load them onto the train. None of us know where the train goes—it's the general consensus, to the extent that there is one, that it would serve no purpose for us to know, and anyway it's not our job. Our job is to collect the souls of the suicides and do everything that comes after.

The soul of a suicide is a delicate thing, a floating wisp of silver gauze, shimmering and nearly transparent. They fall slowly, almost dancing, and sometimes I step outside the dormitories onto the dead grass and I tilt my head back, and I seem to remember something like this once before, catching solid cold on the tip of my tongue.

The soul of a suicide is not cold but gently warm, like the space in a chest where a heart used to nestle. It makes you want to cradle them, gather them close, and sing them songs to which you only know half the words. But we don't hold the suicides like that, because it would show an inappropriate amount of favoritism. We catch them in our huge cloth nets and pull them into the separating trays, where we scoop them up in our hands and wash them in the cloudy water that jets out from the spigots before the trays, and we slide them, softly pulsing, into the collection jars.

When they pulse like that I think of shivering, but I and my fellows never speak about this.

Someone has always been here, doing what we do, because there have always been people who, for one reason or another, decide that life is just not for them. Someone—but it has not always been me. I don't think. Sometimes I lie in my narrow cot in the cavernous dormitory and, like those soft, subtle clouds, I get my fingers around what remains of *before*, but then it slips away and burrows itself into the mud and I don't see it again.

Not until the next time.

‖‖‖‖‖‖‖‖‖‖‖‖‖‖‖‖‖‖‖‖‖

This one had eyes.

In my hands, it blinked up at me. Its eyes were blue and pale, like little fragments of what I remember of a very different sky. There was nothing else of a face on it, but there was all the feeling in the world in those eyes, though there were no tears. I don't know how it blinked, for its eyes were lidless, but there was a flicker in them like a veil passing over and gone again. A veil or part of itself.

I stood there, cradling it in my hands. No one around me seemed to notice, but I was barely aware of that, anyway. The soul of a suicide is not supposed to have eyes. A suicide is done with eyes. As they're done with ears, nose, a mouth. Those were some of the things they relinquished when they gave up everything else. But here it was, looking back at me.

The water was waiting. So was the jar, and then the train. But I didn't move, staring down, and at last I pulled my hands in like the nets, curling them up and over my chest. I held the soul of the suicide close to my unbeating heart, and I slipped it into the folds of my shirt. No one saw me, I don't think. At any rate, no one did anything.

The soul of the suicide pulsed its slow heartbeat pulse. It didn't feel as if it was shivering now.

I know you haven't seen the train of the souls of the suicides. Allow me to describe.

The train is infinite, and none of its cars are ever empty. They contain racks upon racks of our jars, loaded with special mobile arms as it roars past our loading dock in a never-ending rush. It glows in the dimness, and that glow may be individual lights on the outsides of the cars, but with its great speed it appears only as a bright smudged line.

When I'm not collecting or cataloging or loading, I often sit at the dock and watch it, and there are always a few of us off-duty who do the same. There's something fascinating about the train, and also something forbidden, because—again—we don't know and are probably not meant to know where it goes. It races away over the flat, dry land and vanishes over the horizon.

I have had dreams of chasing the train forever, or of loading myself onto it and riding with the suicides. It feels as if it were a thing I was meant to do, and there are times when, watching it go by, the urge to throw myself at it is almost unbearable. Irresistible. I wonder if the others watching with me ever feel the same, but again, this is something about which we don't speak.

But the train of the souls of the suicides is beautiful. I think they might see it as they fall, even without eyes, like a ribbon of silver light in the relative dark.

"Why are you here?"

It was a foolish question. There is only ever one reason why the soul of a suicide is here, and the reason also defines what they are. That final act locking them into one being, forever, or at least until they arrive at whatever destination toward which the train is carrying them. But I sat on my cot and looked down at the soul in my hands, and it looked back up at me. It didn't speak—reasonable, for it had no mouth, but I couldn't help asking anyway.

It was different. It didn't belong.

I heard footsteps and looked up guiltily, but two of my fellows passed me without a glance in my direction. The truth is that we don't often take notice of each other unless something compels us to do so. The place in which we work does not encourage camaraderie.

I'm not sure why I was guilty, why I felt that this was something I should hide, because there is nothing explicitly in the rules about taking a soul from the nets and the separating tables. But perhaps that was why—such a basic rule that it didn't even need to be written down. I did feel as if I was betraying something.

A fine tremble ran through the soul's soft body. I held it close again and closed my eyes.

⁙⁙⁙⁙⁙⁙⁙⁙⁙⁙⁙⁙⁙⁙

We don't catalog names, but reasons and methods.

Common: Long-term depression. Depression that lifts just enough to allow the energy to die. Financial problems. Ruined love. The cruelty of peers. Unemployment. Stress in one's job, education, or other chosen occupation. Loneliness. Shame. The pain of disease. The terror of the future.

All of these things sound so clean when written down and stored in the library, along with catalog numbers and cross-referencing. They sound so simple, so basic. When the truth is that these things are never basic, and the names for what they are disguise the confusion and despair and strange relief of those final moments. What a suicide is, most fundamentally—the act, not just the person who commits it—is the inability to see beyond a moment, a kind of lethal temporal failure of the imagination.

One looks at the future and does not see oneself there, so that ultimate removal is the next logical step.

Suicide is profoundly rational, and we say *commit* because it does indeed require determined intention.

Then of course there are the methods. Common: Cutting of the wrists. Guns. Pills. An overdose of some other drug. Hanging by the neck. Gas. Leaping from a great height—though, as a wise person once observed, it's not the fall that kills you.

Less common is the forcing of the hands of armed law enforcement. Those cases are more complex, and the souls of those suicides don't enter this place alone, though their companions are not our responsibility and so we never see them.

I can recite these things by rote, by memory. I can look at the soul of a suicide and know in an instant what I'm dealing with.

But I didn't know about this one.

I lay curled beneath my covers and I looked at the soul looking back at me with those strange, relentless eyes. I thought of little children reading comic books under the blankets, the image entirely new and coming to me all at once. I leaned my head close so that I could feel its warmth on my cheeks and nose, and I asked, "What happened to you?"

And of course there was no answer, and I didn't get the sense that the soul particularly wanted to tell me. But when I closed my eyes next I felt a sensation of falling, so deep and vivid that it made me gasp. I jerked under the covers, but what I felt wasn't fear but a memory of exhilaration.

A kind of joy.

Suicide by leaping from a great height is my favorite method, if it's appropriate to favor one of these things. It's my favorite because I think of falling as so close to flying, and I wonder if there is no moment at which that soul, trapped in its flesh, hits the ground, but instead breaks free at the instant before impact and continues its descent in a more leisurely fashion, coming into this place and drifting silently toward the ground and our nets. It's a pleasant thought, because it means that some cruelty is left behind before it can be felt, and just because I live in aggregate pain like air doesn't mean that I've lost the ability to feel for what I do.

I have many dreams of flying. It feels like coming home.

I carried the soul of the suicide outside to look up at the sky. It did so, and the quality of its silence changed. I can't say how it was, only that I felt it deeply, with its form in my hands and both of our sets of eyes trained on the falling white of the dead.

It was becoming more solid. If it had been in a jar it could have been contained, but the idea of doing that now was too painful to contemplate. For some reason I couldn't bear the thought of the soul removed from me—since I had last slept I hadn't stopped touching it, hadn't stopped holding it, and setting it down to begin my work was beyond anything I could imagine. I could feel possibilities foreclosing themselves on me. I could feel the future narrowing.

I hadn't ever really thought about the future.

"You came from there," I said, as if speaking to a child, and then, to underscore both the point and the attitude, I gestured to the drifting souls. "Do you remember? Do you remember how it happened, can you tell me why you're here?"

No answer. But again it trembled, and now I was sure that it wanted to tell me something, and the fact that it couldn't was a strange, choked kind of agony. I held my breath and looked anywhere but at it, because all at once its gaze felt like something that could tear me open and reveal something I wasn't ready to see.

Sometimes one of us disappears. Our terms here are finite, we all know that. We don't remember how we came to be here, and we don't know where we're going when our work here is complete, but none of us are afraid. There's nothing to fear in this place. Your heart might hurt, but your body is invincible.

I don't know if I want to go. I can't imagine anything other than this. Even the possibility of the train is a blank, and extends no further than as far as you can travel before you lose sight of the loading dock, the nets, the library, and the dormitories.

It isn't real.

I wandered the places where I used to work. No one called to me or ordered me to take my place or demanded an explanation, so I had long since lost my guilt at my inability to perform my duties. No one even looked up at me as I passed them, and I began to feel unreal myself, as gauzy and indistinct as the soul I carried against my chest. But the soul was still solidifying, its surface becoming smooth and supple like flesh and skin, its pulsing like a beating heart rather than just the memory of one. I held it close to me and I felt something in my chest, long still, wanting to move in response.

What becomes of the body of a suicide? Of course there's undressing, washing, cutting, the draining of the blood and other fluids, and perhaps a dusting of makeup, maybe the tears of loved ones left behind, and then the ground or the fire. I know that once some people interred their dead in silent towers, offerings to the birds of the air. There's something deeply romantic about that idea, and though I don't suppose it's common anymore, I do wish it remained as a practice, the bodies of the suicides divided fairly among winged things and carried into the sky to fly in their warm bellies, cradled beneath their fluttering hearts.

But what becomes of the body of a suicide, after all of this is done? Are they also set aside, like their souls? Is the manner of the dissolution particular, or in that are they like all the other dead? I have heard it said that death is a great equalizer, but every passing moment I see evidence to the contrary. Does this rule extend to the flesh?

I feel like it should. I look for evidence of that as well, and though I see none, it's a belief of which I can't rid myself. The bodies of the suicides go somewhere specific, fallen to pieces but still bound together. Perhaps they lie in silent tombs, holding their rage and their grief in each cell until those cells finally break down into atoms and rejoin the stars. But are those stars particular as well? Do they become the dying stars? Do they become lonely dwarf stars, pulsars beating like hearts? Do they enjoy the drama of the supernova? Or do they drift, ordinary, to join suns like the one I almost remember?

Do they go somewhere else? Do they still have work to do?

||||||||||||||||||||||||||||||

I carried the soul of the suicide through the library. I felt its eyes scanning the massive wooden shelves of records, taking stock of each part of the stacks. I told it stories of the things I've cataloged, the things I've seen. As I did this I felt its trembling intensifying, its eyes wanting to turn away, and at last I stopped, holding it up before my face. The library is lit by great red paper lanterns, their sides decorated with script I have never known how to read. In that light, I saw the flesh of the soul knitting itself together, and I saw blood moving sluggishly through its network of veins.

I pulled in a long breath. I have no heartbeat but I can feel my lungs expand and contract, because I have that much life left in me. I held the soul of the suicide up to the lights like an offering, and I felt my throat closing up, leaving only a narrow passage for the air to travel through.

"Tell me," I whispered. "I want to help you." But the soul of the suicide simply looked at me, its eyes huge and sad, and in that look was all the longing for what it couldn't say.

I tightened my hands around it, this thing that had pulled me from my work, that had opened and closed these doors to me. I wanted to crush it, tear at it, throw it onto the floor and stomp it into paste. But instead I embraced it again and clenched my teeth, and tears were something else that was new to me, and unwelcome, burning on my cold cheeks.

I should never have lifted the soul out of the net.

But I could never have done anything else.

<hr />

I never wanted to remember. Like the train, it's always been easier to know only a little. I never wanted to plumb the logic of things, to search and to seek and to find. I never wanted to be given answers. I was content with ignorance, with only enough information to perform my work to the best of my ability.

But then, when I lay awake in my bed with the dormitory all silent and dark around me, the soul burrowed into my chest.

I could feel it breaking me open. There was no pain, but I could feel the parting of my skin, the cracking of my breastbone. I stiffened, but I didn't pull away. I felt warm flesh nosing into me, nuzzling like a loving thing. I felt those fine trembles against my lungs. I felt it nudging my silent heart carefully aside. I felt it settling there, softly insistent, and I felt how perfectly it fit. I turned my head, arcing upward, and I felt myself falling, falling, falling forever, turning in something like a soul's dance as I tore open and leaped free.

I and not I.

And then I understood.

The why doesn't matter. Sit in this stillness, let the pain settle around you like a blanket. This moment, this penultimate moment, and the sky is calling. There is so much comfort in a decision, a final grab for power. You can still make choices, and this feels like the most meaningful one you have ever made. You don't even remember what brought you to this point anymore. Everything around you is stripping itself away. You can feel yourself pulling apart. You can feel yourself aching for something through the air that gathers itself around your heart. You can imagine nothing beyond this, except the moment your heart stops beating, and it feels like love. The ground will embrace you. Throw your head back. Cherish these breaths. Feel so incredibly alive. Listen to the singing birds, the rough cries of the crows. They might even catch you; you don't really understand how this works anyway, except you know it's easy.

And we are always in pieces. We are born in pieces and we can't do anything but die that way.

So go to the door in the world. Your escape hatch. Shed everything else like an old skin. Put your faith in gravity, which will certainly not let you down.

Fly.

So now I wait on the loading dock. I am in one piece, and in pieces. I have been waiting for this moment for so long, but I don't really know how long, and it might only be a moment or two. It was very easy to wait, but very hard to let it happen, harder than it should have been, but I think maybe it's always this hard for us. I know that no one around me even sees me anymore. I am contained, in my own little invisible jar that is also flesh and bones that is the culmination of a choice that is everything I am.

I look at the infinite rush of the train, the roaring of a monster of light, but now it sounds like birdsong. A massive bird, claws open to catch me.

And I can't see beyond this moment.

This is something I never understood: It's not even that you can't see beyond the moment. It's the leap that takes you through that inability to see, the leap that is all the faith you can muster. A desperate attempt at escape. And it breaks you apart, but in the end you come together again.

I might be a star. I might. But right now my heart is hot and beating in time with the rhythm of the train of the souls of the suicides, and I will know my own destination. I will make this choice. I will take a leap of faith.

My eyes are open when I jump.

They always were.

THE THROAT IS DEEP AND THE MOUTH IS WIDE

|||||||||||||||||||||||||||||||||||||||||||||||||||||||||||||||||||||||||||||||

THIS ONE DOESN'T WANT A CONVERSATION.

It's creepy. Or once I would have thought that. But now it's a matter of course. There are hundreds of these. Probably thousands, counting the ones who never come to me. It's not creepy, not really.

It makes me feel so goddamn sad.

He only wants me to whisper. He pays for an hour, talks quietly and haltingly. He stutters a little; I can tell he's not used to this yet. He doesn't want to see my face or my lips. Doesn't want the experience of reading facial expressions, body language. Shape of mouth, lift of brow. Set of shoulders. Eyes. Head tilt.

No. Just voice.

Goodnight, I whisper. Over and over, exactly like he's paying me to do. I drift to his eardrum and I caress, soothe; I coax my way deeper and he receives me. I have no idea what's inside this man's head. He sounds young, even by outbound standards. He sounds terrified. I have go to bed tonight knowing that he'll probably always be terrified now, and no amount of gentle verbal exhalation is going to help him. Five years ago a hole opened up in the universe roughly at the midpoint between Earth and the Moon, and like so many others since then, it ate him. I can't change that.

But this is something I can do.

I'm not supposed to get emotionally tangled up in clients, but fuck that. I guess.

Goodnight. Goodnight. Goodnight.

⸻

Outbound. Months in the dark. Sometimes—rarely—years. No one knows why the spaces into which the inexplicable portal deposits its travelers eat the light the way they do. No one knows much about it at all. What we know is that it's not normal space in the sense we understand, and it's not at all safe. It takes a very, very long time to get there and get back. A lot of people never do.

The people who do... About thirty percent of them come back *knowing* things.

The first one through returned with fully accurate knowledge of his own personal future, extending about a year before it abruptly cut off and his perception was once again confined to the present and the past. It fucked him up, badly—he committed suicide a couple of weeks after he lost the future—but it was enough to get other people up and moving. People wanting to know things they had no other way of knowing. *What happened to this person I lost. What's going to happen to me and him/her/they. Will I ever realize my dreams. Is she cheating on me. Is he in love with me. Are they truly my child. Who have I been, what will I be. What will I become. What can I do. What should I do. How do I do anything.*

The outbound go out, if they're lucky their heads are stuffed full of information, the presence of which no one can understand or explain, and they come back.

They come back insane.

A little. A lot. Even if you come back with nothing, you're insane. At the very least you're wobbling along the edge of sanity. You'd think that would deter people, but no: there is, in the ones who go, an insatiable desire to *know*.

But it's never knowledge that would be useful to anyone else. It's never history, or science, or philosophy. It's never any kind of Ultimate Truth. It's selfish. Purely and brutally so.

More than once I've wondered if they went out there because they were batshit crazy to begin with.

⁂

Months alone in the dark, no instrumentation, no illumination of any kind. You live on nutrient fluids and hyper-compressed dry rations. You bathe with a sponge. You spend a month of lengthy training sessions in your transport, your pod, learning every centimeter of it by touch.

The hole and the space beyond don't eat the sound. But the darkness seems to, in some kind of fundamental way entirely to do with perception. People come back and they need to talk to someone, anyone; they need to hear a voice. More than they need to see. Most of them actually prefer complete darkness. But they need to be spoken to. Sung to. They need to go to sleep to endless, repetitive bedtime stories.

Recorded voices don't work. They also don't seem to help the outbound while they're out. As with so much of this, no one is sure why. There's something about externality and sentience; a human voice in the void with you and on the other end of that connection. These people need whispers in the endless dark that's settled itself into the expanses between their altered synapses.

They need to know they still have a present. They need to know they're *here*. A touch. A tether. That seems simple. So I took this job because it was something I could do.

I set my own hours. I can also work from anywhere, technically, since all I need is a data connection and audio. But this isn't the kind of thing you do in public. Or I don't. I tried once or twice, because it seemed more convenient, if I could make it practical. Go out, go to the park, cafes, walk around and look at things and maybe talk to people—the stuff you're supposed to do in order to be a well-adjusted human being alive in the world. But when I tried it felt like fucking in the middle of the street. It felt awkward. Creepy. I was sitting at a table in a coffee shop and my skin started crawling.

I took the call because I knew she didn't want me to do anything too raw. She just wanted to chat. About what she was up to, how she's been settling back into her house and getting some renovations done. About streams she likes—turns out we liked a couple of the same ones. About nothing. The business of *being*. There was nothing to overhear, if anyone wanted to eavesdrop.

But I couldn't do it. It felt obscene. It still does a lot of the time—sometimes it *is*, depending on what people seem to need—but in private it's easier.

So I set my own hours, but I also don't go out much anymore.

****

I tend to put myself on-call late at night, my time. I don't know what it is, but the words flow easier and with less concentration, which means the sessions tend to be less exhausting. But late at night—though granted, the specific provider that employs me is global and some of the people who call aren't anywhere near my timezone—is when things also tend to get weird.

I don't mean sexual stuff. I mean, there *is* more of that, and it *is* often less conventional. But I mean *weird*. People call and they just *breathe*, there's very little info in their profile to guide me, and I flail around, trying to hit on anything they might want. Or they want to perform for me—sing songs they wrote or poetry they've written and get honest critiques. Or they want me to play some kind of role for them, and the roles are disturbing.

I can't complain. I put myself in this position. For some reason I haven't articulated to myself, I prefer it. But I don't *like* it, and every second I'm on-call my stomach twists itself into tighter and tighter knots, birthing slow nausea.

Sometimes I feel the persistent suspicion that I'm looking for something. Waiting for something specific to come along. I have no idea how I would know it when it comes. But I keep going, held fast to it. My own tether is to some unspecified future, and that's unsettling.

There are things I don't know, and I don't know if I wish I could.

I wander the apartment, watching the yellow and black stripe-shadows from the half open blinds float across my skin. I am a bee in the dark. I'm buzzing to unseen companions. We spin through a cold, starless void and now and then we orbit each other. But gravity always flings us away again, and in the end I'm as lost as they are.

Four AM. Stream on mute, whiskey. I shouldn't drink on the job and if somehow I were caught I would be fined per my contract, but I just got done with a two hour session of... People joke about *mommy issues, daddy issues.* I think they joke because those issues are completely universal—literally, and it seems like months of near-sensory deprivation make those issues a hell of a lot worse. Even worse when you come back and discover Mommy and/or Daddy are dead, and there are things you want to say to them.

Anyway. That's why I'm drinking.

But I'm still on-call. So when I'm called, if the profile doesn't make it clear that I absolutely can't handle it, I have to take it.

This is a woman. Three years younger than me. Went out, came back, didn't know anything. The dates of departure and return and that's all. That she's a woman, and a couple of numbers that tell me essentially nothing.

*Don't take the call. Come up with an excuse. You can do that,
you think on your feet for a living.*

Low voice, soothing, smooth, utterly neutral. Default Mode.
And no *hi, you've reached the* _____ *foundation/corporation/
organization*. Nothing to indicate the financial nature of this
transaction. From the second I take the call, I'm spinning a carefully flexible web of artifice and make-believe.

"Hey, how's it going? Do you need to talk to someone?"

Nothing on the other end of the line, and at first I think it's
another breather, which I simply do not know if I can handle.
But then, a voice just as low as mine.

"Yeah."

"I'm here to talk. Whatever you need. Is there something in
particular you'd like to talk about?" A little brisker than normal,
if I'm honest, but now that this has started, I want it over as soon
as possible.

Nothing again. Then, "I...I don't know. I've never done this."

"Doesn't have to be anything specific." Vague would have
been exasperating. New, I can work with. "Is something on your
mind?"

"I don't know." A shaky breath, and words all in a rush, tumbling end over end. "I just...I don't know, I haven't talked to anyone in months, I don't...I don't know if I can do this, I'm sorry."

Freshly inbound. Her profile said.

"You don't have to do anything. If you need to hear someone
talk, I can take care of that. I can read to you, or there are things
I can tell you about. Would any—"

"Tell me about your sister."

I drop my own sentence and I merely sit there in the dark, and
her last words hang in that darkness with me. I'm staring at it. It
rotates slowly, shadowy, like a planet far removed from its star.

"I don't have a sister."

"No?" Her voice is so low it's almost inaudible. "Oh. All right.
I'm sorry."

And she's gone.

⸺

Sometimes the people who go out make their aims known. Sometimes they want everyone to know what they're looking for, what secret is dragging them into the dark. More often they go out with that secret firmly kept so. That's why it's a secret to begin with. If they come back knowing.

Hell. We don't know how many come back knowing things and never tell. All we know about are the crazy ones. Those are the only ones we can count.

Sometimes it can kill you, wondering what they wanted. Wondering what they needed to know that badly. Sometimes it keeps you up at night. Keeps you on-call, because there's no point in letting your damn brain whirl like a hurricane.

We don't ask. We're not allowed to ask. For whatever reason, they never volunteer the information. But you wonder.

Maybe you're waiting for the one time that changes.

⸺

Something that interested me—kind of surprised me—when I started out in this job is that you actually *don't* get a whole lot of repeat business. For the most part when someone calls you once you don't hear from them again. Maybe once or twice more, but nothing else. It's an interesting contrast with what I understand traditional therapy is like: you form a relationship with someone, you reveal a long strand of history beaded with problems and you work through it together, fingering every bead like a rosary, praying for healing. Absolution. Your sin was sentience. The fall of self-awareness.

These people don't want to be self-aware. They had months in the dark to become aware of themselves. So you don't form an attachment. You don't let anyone get to know you that well. You confess but you don't pray. This therapy is all one night stands.

It's not just for them. We see the same profile pop up more than once, we have the option of referring. It's not good for business if we're being forced into emotional bonds we don't want and can't control.

You can't get attached to someone you can't save.

Rain. The streetlights outside catch the drops on the window, illuminate them like flowing balls of mercury. Every trickle on the glass a river. I map them, and when her profile comes up I don't refer, and I have no idea why.

I really fucking should.

"Hi. Do you need to talk to someone?"

"Yeah. I...I think so. Yes." As uncertain as before...And also not so much. She sounds more *there* than she did. She's not just listening on the other end. She sounds like she might be able to reach. "I can't sleep."

So she's in my time zone. Probably. Actually, who the hell knows; I get the distinct sense that the people who call me—like me—don't maintain a conventional circadian rhythm.

"What are you thinking about?"

There's a long silence. Then, quietly: "Do you think everyone has a moment where...when they realize that someday everyone they love is going to be gone?"

It's not the weirdest question I've ever been asked. I lay a hand on the window, watch rivers of rain vanish into my fingertips. "I don't know. Did you have one?"

"I don't remember one. I don't remember when I knew. It just happened." Another pause. Her voice hasn't increased in volume, but it sounds clearer, as if she's moved into an area with better reception. "I think I had to lose someone before it was real. It happens once, it can happen anytime. You think about little kids at the funerals of grandparents. A body is just a body, no matter how much makeup they cake on. Little kids are little but they aren't stupid. They know the person is gone. They're looking at a thing. Suddenly it's right in front of them, solid enough to touch. Maybe they don't completely understand it at the time, but the seed gets planted. It sprouts. Every time it happens. Every time you lose someone else."

I don't completely follow what she's saying. That's also not unusual. But I don't like it. It's *not* like usual, and I'd like it to stop. As I suspected I might, I'm wishing I had just referred. "So you lost someone? Was it a grandparent?"

"I lost everyone."

This is common among people who come back, regardless of what they know. The isolation. The inability to connect, to reconnect with people with whom they shared the deepest possible connections. They know there's a good chance of this and it doesn't seem to matter to them.

"Can you tell me how?"

More silence. Then I hear it: an odd clicking. A crackle. As if that good reception is gone.

"The usual. Space, Lonnie. Space and time."

We never tell them our names. Ever.

I have no idea what the fuck I would say, if I could move my lips. My tongue. Every nerve ending just quit on me. Refused to accept any more input.

Wouldn't matter anyway. She's gone. For real this time.

For real.

||||||||||||||||||||||||||||||

She calls a third time, two days later. We get as far as the introductory lines, there's about a minute of silence, then she cuts the call.

||||||||||||||||||||||||||||||

I've never wanted to quit. I've never actually wanted to stop doing this. Not that I love it. Work like this has a kind of inertia. It's difficult for me, now, to imagine doing anything else. That's not a problem, but it's a thing.

Honestly sometimes I have a hard time remembering when I did anything else. What it was like. What I used to want to do. What I used to want. What I want now. What I'm waiting for. Whether maybe I was hoping I might find something.

Whether something happened that made me forget.

I sit and I try to remember. The non-sound of an open line is like a conch shell full of darkness. There used to be something there. There might be again. What you're listening to is the sound of alternates. Every possible voice. So many. This one keeps coming back.

In that darkness, something moves.

⠀⠀⠀⠀⠀⠀⠀⠀⠀⠀⠀⠀⠀⠀⠀⠀⠀⠀⠀⠀⠀⠀⠀⠀⠀⠀⠀⠀⠀⠀⠀⠀⠀⠀⠀

I sit by the window with the phone set to on-call and I watch the rain. I do this for hours. The rain continues for those hours. Longer. It rained yesterday, and the day previous. I'm having difficulty remembering what I did before this; I'm also having difficulty remembering what the world was like when it wasn't raining. Sunlight instead of this endless low gray. Color instead of monochrome. I stare, and sometimes blinking becomes an afterthought and when at last I do, my eyes burn and sting with dry-air grit.

I don't have the past anymore. I'm not sure about the *now*.

I've dealt with my share of problematic clients, but this one is different and I have no idea how to explain it to myself. I don't want to avoid this girl. I don't want to refer her. I could. I don't actually need the money that badly and it's not like I can't pick up another one. I have scores. But I don't want to, so I don't.

I want her to call. Want to know if she will.

The sun lost behind the clouds goes down. In the dark, I'm waiting, and I haven't spoken to her in three days.

In these moments of deep waiting, poised on the edge and ready to be knocked over into the abyss when what you're waiting for finally goes down, they stretch out and out and you occupy them like a pocket universe. They enfold you. Everything is about one single thing. You don't remember a before and it's difficult to imagine an after. You wait and you want and it consumes you.

I'm having trouble remembering familiar faces in any detail. I'm having trouble remembering the names of my old friends, the ones I'm still in contact with. Or was. I'm losing myself and it doesn't panic me. It's like watching from a distance, separate from the self I've become. I've split off because there isn't enough room in that pocket universe for more than a small fragment of *I*.

I've been here before. Sitting in the dark, blinds drawn now against a wet night. Touching my cheeks and brow and nose and chin, weirdly fascinated by the structure of my own bones, which I've had forever but which I suspect may be like a word repeated until it becomes strange, feeling and sounding alien in the mouth and ears. I've been here in this capsule, and I know what it's like to wait for a call that won't come.

I know what it's like to be tired of waiting.

⊞⊞⊞⊞⊞⊞⊞⊞⊞⊞⊞

I don't remember picking up the call. I don't remember checking the ID info or glancing at the dossier. I don't remember making the decision to do it, to do anything. I don't remember these things because I don't need to, because the motivations for a thing ultimately don't matter once the thing is happening.

This is the nature of the present.

I read a piece once on some science site or other about how we make decisions. About how we don't *make* them at all, at least not the way we like to think we do. About how we just *do* shit—we see a collection of options in front of us and we lunge for one according to a logic far beneath anything we're conscious of, and once it's been done and we can look back at it with a minute or two of hindsight, we come up with the thought process that led us there. We construct something that never existed in the first place, like looking back at the river you've crossed and building the bridge so you can understand how you got there.

I don't make the decision. I'm just taking the call, and I'm floating in the dark and as always I'm waiting.

"Lonnie?"

Lifting my hand, turning my fingers against the streaks of rain-light on the window. Streaks but also beads; caught like they are, they look like stars. Close enough to be spherical, suspended on a transparent membrane. "I'm here."

"I know you are." She's silent. Dead air. Then, "What do you want, Lonnie?"

No decision to make. "I don't know."

Lost in the dark, waiting to be found. In the end a voice is all I had. I don't have light. On a call, my body doesn't matter. It has no part in the connection I'm making, the connection I have to make. There are my lungs, my vocal cords, teeth and tongue and lips, but after long enough you stop noticing those.

In the end, without a voice, I'm nothing.

"Did you come here to find out?" She takes a breath, slow. It sounds like wind in trees. I think of the spreading branches of bronchi, red like autumns I can barely recall. They flare with the inward rush of oxygen and fade as it leaves them.

Things happen and we only make sense of them after, if we make sense of them at all. We always want to know, we want to know everything, but I think what we want to know more than anything else is *why*. They never ask me, but I think it was behind every word they said and every word they asked me to say.

It happens, and you only find out after. *Gone.* And she never said. And you don't know why.

"I can't explain that."

"No, Lonnie. You can't."

"What do *you* want?" I'm tight with sudden desperation. I've been waiting and it's been here the whole time, but it keeps slipping away. I just wanted to know. Every voice, maybe this would be the one who could tell me. I don't want the past or the present or the future. I don't want anything that complicated.

"I don't want anything."

"Everyone wants something." They do. I've learned that. It's one of the few things I know. "That's why they call."

"That's why they're here in the first place. But they don't want what they want, Lonnie. That's why they always go back empty. Even when they have something, they go back empty. They need to be filled and they have no idea with what, and that's why they call you. They reach out to you because they want to know what they wanted in the first place, and they don't have any answers. They won't even talk to themselves anymore. When they went out, that was taken from them. They didn't think about the choice so they didn't know what they were giving up." She pauses again, and I listen to the wind. "And they look back and there's no bridge. There isn't even a river. There's just the dark."

"Nothing makes sense." I can't get it above a whisper but I know she hears. It's silent here. There's nothing to drown me out.

"There's no way to *make* it make sense. But none of the rest of them ever came back out. When you're inbound you're inbound forever. Except you."

"I didn't-"

"Why are you different, Lonnie?"

I make a fist and hold it up. The bronchi, the heart. In the light through the rain, it looks like I'm pulsing. Beating. "You *know* why. Christ, you should know that better than *anyone.* They didn't lose what I lost."

"You don't know what you lost."

"*You.*"

Oh.

I'm breaking open. I was always open; I'm coalescing. Collapsing. "I just wanted to know. What happened. Why. Why can't I know that? It wasn't selfish. It *wasn't for me.*" Why couldn't they understand that? Waiting for news, for one specific inbound pod, day after day after day, and in the end there was nothing, and no one could ever tell me *what happened.* No one could ever tell me *why.*

What she wanted to know.

She's fading. The color is receding, the wind leaving and taking it along, and the orbit is swinging outward again. Eventually she'll slingshot away, go floating off into nothing and I won't have her voice anymore.

I won't know any more than she probably did.

Unless she knew everything. Unless that's why she never came back.

"Reason isn't resurrection, Lonnie. You can't change something when you understand why it happened. And it won't fill the empty place inside. You came back with it still empty, but you would have even if you knew."

"But even that wasn't why. Not really."

Why?

You just couldn't take the silence any longer.

||||||||||||||||||||||||||

Sitting alone in the dark, dead air in my ear. All around. This is what I'm left with. Nothing is better, nothing makes sense, and she's gone. I don't know when she hung up. I don't know what the last thing she said to me was. I don't know what I was waiting for, whether I got any part of it. I don't know anything.

That's the point.

We all have that moment, that one moment that stands like a threshold between a child and an adult, when we realize everyone we love is going to be gone.

We all have that moment when we realize everyone we love already is.

Why makes no difference. The ones who come back with it aren't any luckier than the ones who don't, because in the dark and the silence, what you *know* doesn't make you less alone.

Hey. How's it going?

Do you need to talk to someone?

PUBLICATION HISTORY

"A Perdition of Salt," and "The Throat is Deep and the Mouth is Wide" are original to this collection.

"Come My Love and I'll Tell You a Tale," originally appeared in *Shimmer* #24, March 2015; "Singing With All My Skin and Bone," originally appeared in *Nightmare* #24, Sept. 2014; "Cold As the Moon," originally appeared in *Strange Horizons*, Aug. 2014; "I Tell Thee All, I Can No More," originally appeared in *Clarkesworld* #82, July 2013; "Across the Seam," originally appeared in *Long Hidden: Speculative Fiction From the Margins of History*, 2015; "Dispatches From a Hole in the World ," originally appeared in *Nightmare* #37: *Queers Destroy Horror!*, Oct. 2015; "Event Horizon," originally appeared in *Strange Horizons*, Oct. 2013; "The Horse Latitudes," originally appeared in *Ideomancer*, Vol. 12, Issue 1, 2013; "All the Literati Keep An Imaginary Friend," originally appeared in *Murmuration: A Festival of Drone Culture*, June 2013; "Love Letters to Things Lost and Gained," originally appeared in *Uncanny* #2, Jan. 2015; "Memento Mori," originally appeared in *Shadows & Tall Trees* #2, Aug. 2011; "The Cold Death of Papa November," originally appeared in *Three-Lobed Burning Eye* #21, Sept. 2011; "So Sharp That Blood Must Flow," originally appeared in *Lightspeed* #45, Feb. 2014; "Tell Me How All This (And Love Too) Will Ruin Us," originally appeared in *Daily Science Fiction*, Nov. 2013; "Love in the Time of Vivisection," originally appeared in *Shimmer* #17, Sept. 2013; "A Shadow on the Sky," originally appeared in *Mythic Delrium* 1.3, Feb. 2015; "It is Healing, It Is Never Whole," originally appeared in *Apex* #75, Aug. 2015.

Sunny Moraine's short fiction has appeared in *Clarkesworld, Strange Horizons, Nightmare, Lightspeed, Long Hidden: Speculative Fiction from the Margins of History*, and multiple Year's Best anthologies, among other places. They are also responsible for the *Root Code* and *Casting the Bones* trilogies and the novels *Labyrinthian* and *Lineage*, as well as *A Brief History of the Future: collected essays*. In addition to time spent authoring, Sunny is a doctoral candidate in sociology and a sometime college instructor; that last may or may not have been a good move on the part of their department. They unfortunately live just outside Washington, DC, in a creepy house with two cats and a very long-suffering husband.

YEAR'S BEST
WEIRD FICTION
VOLUME ONE

EDITED BY
LAIRD BARRON
AND MICHAEL KELLY

Year's Best Weird Fiction, Volume One

"Well, it's a triumph. A really well-assembled collection,
which succeeds in distinguishing itself from the best horror and
best fantasy anthologies with an eclectic table of contents."

—Nathan Ballingrud, author of North American Lake Monsters

Oct. 2014   www.undertowbooks.com

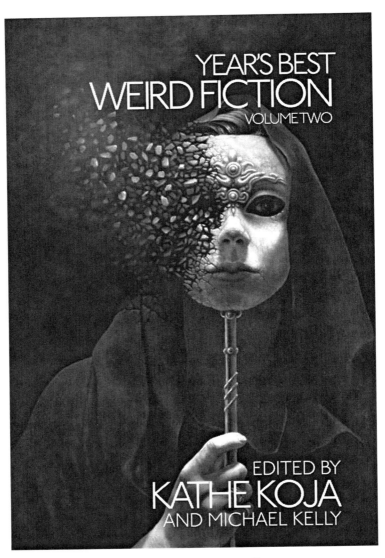

YEAR'S BEST
WEIRD FICTION
VOLUME TWO

EDITED BY
KATHE KOJA
AND MICHAEL KELLY

Year's Best Weird Fiction, Volume Two

"Weird fiction . . . the plexus that knits together fantasy and horror and
creates an ever-changing whole, remarkable for its very mutability.

—Laird Barron

October 2015   www.undertowbooks.com

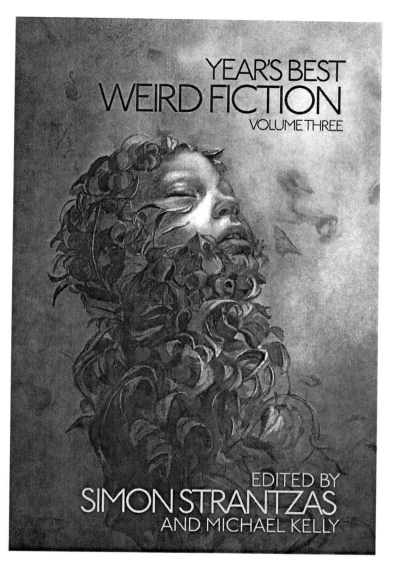

YEAR'S BEST
WEIRD FICTION
VOLUME THREE

EDITED BY
SIMON STRANTZAS
AND MICHAEL KELLY

Year's Best Weird Fiction, Volume Three

Forthcoming, October 2016   www.undertowbooks.com

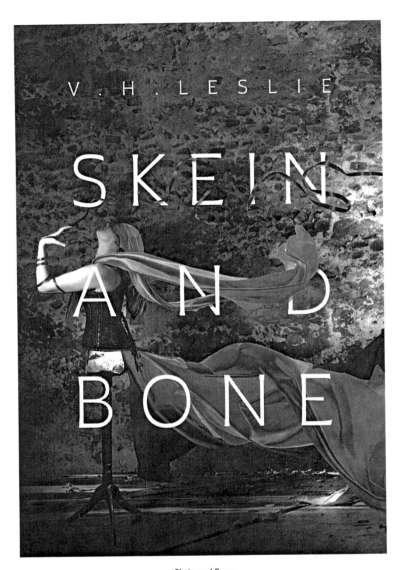

Skein and Bone

"An absorbing and gorgeously unsettling collection."

—Alison Moore, The Lighthouse, (Short-Listed for the Man-Booker)

August 2015   www.undertowbooks.com

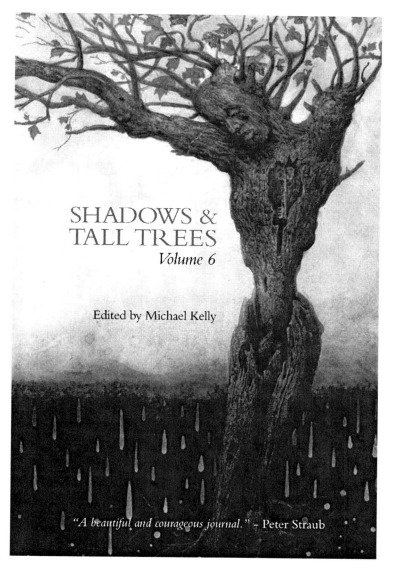

SHADOWS &
TALL TREES
Volume 6

Edited by Michael Kelly

"A beautiful and courageous journal." – Peter Straub

Shadows & Tall Trees, Volume 6

(Shirley Jackson Award Nominee, Edited Anthology)

"A beautiful and courageous volume."

—Peter Straub, author of Ghost Story

March 2014   www.undertowbooks.com

Meet Me in The Middle of The Air

"Showcases stories both horrific and transgressive . . . "

—Jeff VanderMeer, Best-Selling Author of the *Southern Reach* trilogy

February 2016   www.undertowbooks.com

CPSIA information can be obtained
at www.ICGtesting.com
Printed in the USA
LVOW11s1532281016

510723LV00003B/473/P